Girls Dinner Club

Girls Dinner Club

Jessie Elliot

HarperCollinsPublishers

 Produced by Alloy Entertainment
151 West 26th Street, New York, NY 10001

Library of Congress Cataloging-in-Publication Data

Elliot, Jessie.
 Girls dinner club / Jessie Elliot.— 1st ed.
  p. cm.
 Summary: Junie, Celia, and Danielle, three ethnically diverse
high schoolers in Brooklyn, form a friendship while cooking
dinners together and helping one another sort through their romantic
entanglements.
 ISBN 0-06-059539-6 — ISBN 0-06-059540-X (lib. bdg.)
 [1. Friendship—Fiction. 2. Cookery—Fiction. 3. Interpersonal
relations—Fiction. 4. Brooklyn (New York, N.Y.)—Fiction.]
I. Title.
PZ7.E432Gi 2005   2004021504
[Fic]—dc22

Typography by Christopher Grassi
1 2 3 4 5 6 7 8 9 10
❖
First Edition

For Julie B.

Girls Dinner Club

Monsoons,
Marathons,
and
Massages

A week and a half of relentless rain and Junie Wong-Goldstein was going out of her skull with stir-craziness. It had been one of those weird springs more suited to Seattle than Brooklyn: gloomy skies, angry winds, and passionate, basement-flooding downpours. The track team had been running indoors, lap after lap around the cinder-block gym. On Tuesday, Coach had canceled practice altogether; the boys' team needed the gym for an extended workout.

"So let's run outside," Brian said, waiting at Junie's locker for her to pack up her books. Brian was her boyfriend of almost a year, always good for a wacky idea.

"No way. It's monsooning out there." Junie, one of the top female sprinters in the Brooklyn High School Athletic League, ran five miles a day as a matter of habit. Heat, snow, fog, wind—no meteorological phenomenon could stop her, except for heavy rain. She hated to run in the rain. Her sneakers sloshed, her shorts glued themselves to her thighs, and she always ended up with water in her ears.

"Don't be a wimp," Brian said. He'd just gotten out of gym and was still wearing shorts, plus a white T-shirt and one of the thread necklaces Junie braided for him when she got bored in precalculus class.

"We'll catch pneumonia," she said.

"You sound like my mother," he said.

From the look on Brian's face, she could tell he wasn't about to be swayed. "Oh, fine." She shrugged. The run would break the monotony of the past week and a half, and besides, she needed the exercise. She followed Brian out of Brooklyn Prep and into the deluge. She wished she wasn't wearing jeans. Rain poured off the high school's front awning in sheets.

"On your mark, get set . . ." And he was off.

"This is so insane!" Junie shouted as she chased him down Brooklyn Prep's front lawn, her sneakers squeaking in the mud. She watched as his T-shirt grew translucent, exposing his freckled back with the tattoo of the dancing bear. She was glad she was wearing a black tank.

"Let's go, Goldstein! No chatter!" Brian barked. They turned down Sixth Avenue, dodging fire hydrants, parking meters, and umbrella-toting shoppers who stared at them as if they were crazy. Even though Brian was more than a foot taller than she was—six-one to Junie's five-foot-nothing—she pumped her arms harder and soon caught up with him. She squeezed her eyes shut against the downpour and felt her ponytail drip water down her back.

"You know, it's at least five miles to my house," she said.

"Not a problem," Brian said, sailing over a pile of dog crap on the sidewalk.

They ran past the fruit stores and coffee shops of Bay Ridge and alongside the Chinese and Latino groceries of Sunset Park. Rain plastered Brian's blond hair to his forehead and ran in rivulets down the backs of his knees. He took off his shirt and tossed it in a garbage bin.

With Junie in the lead, they turned into the vast Green-Wood Cemetery and skirted the ancient gravestones. The willow trees in the cemetery were sagging with the weight of the rain, but Junie was starting to really enjoy herself. The exercise, the oxygen, the clean air on her skin—it all felt deliriously sweet, even though her backpack was soaked and her sneakers were flooded. "How you doing?" she called over her shoulder.

"All good." Brian shook the water off his head like a wet cat.

"Want to take a break?"

"Breaks are for losers," he said, and sprinted ahead, trying to pass her on the left. His messenger bag flopped along his side.

"I don't think so!" Junie shrieked, reaching out to tickle him. He caught her, kissed her, and then let her go. This was the most fun they'd had together in weeks.

Out of the cemetery, up Fifth Avenue, turning down Ninth Street, making a right on Smith, and then up through Carroll Gardens. Past the Italian bakeries, the grand old churches, the hipster bars, the park. A left on Bergen Street.

Past the first stoplight. And then they arrived, finally, soaked to the skin and panting. Junie's enormous nineteenth-century brownstone, where the porch lights were always on and nobody was ever home.

"That was excellent," Brian said, drying his shaggy hair with his hands. They had tossed their clothes into the dryer and were wearing Junie's parents' fluffy bathrobes, lying on their king-sized bed, listening to the Shins. Junie's parents traveled so much that she slept in their room most nights; their bed was softer and bigger and their walls were wired with surround sound. Brian had hooked up her iPod to their speakers.

"I think we made pretty good time, too, considering." She tilted her head and smacked her hand against her ear. "That should be a new Olympic event. The monsoon marathon."

"Or it could be one of those ESPN extreme sports," Brian said. "They could have it in India, during the rainy season." India was one of Brian's obsessions. The others were Phish, Frisbee, snowboarding, and Junie.

"Ooh, that's a good idea. And they could use underwater cameras to record it. And everybody could run in wet suits."

"And they'd have to swim through rivers and stuff. Dodge crocodiles."

"Or piranhas."

"Or gun-wielding political insurgents." Brian sat up, took one of Junie's feet in his hands, and began to rub.

4

"Like a combination X Game, international-crisis-type sporting event," Junie said, leaning back and closing her eyes. Brian gave the best foot rubs in the world. "Thanks for making me run," she said. "I needed it."

"I could tell." Brian pressed the ball of her foot. "You've seemed pretty stressed out lately." He moved his thumb in circles and then climbed his hands up her ankle to her calf. He rubbed first her right leg, then her left.

"Oh my God, that feels so good." She sank drowsily into her parents' jumbo silk pillows, stuffed fat with goose down.

Brian kept rubbing her left calf, and then slowly moved his hands up to her knee, and then her lower thigh. He stayed there for a while before starting to move his hands upward again. Junie didn't want to protest—it felt too great—although she couldn't help worrying about exactly where he was going with this massage. She kept her eyes closed, but she could feel his hands moving up, up, up. He tugged at her underwear. She jerked her leg away.

"What?"

"I just don't feel like doing that right now," Junie said. "I'm kind of . . . tired."

"Tired?" Brian said. "Really?" He lay down next to her and put his head on the same pillow. "Don't be tired," he said, tracing her jawline with his finger. They kissed for a while, and soon Junie's heart started to beat faster, not because of any particular excitement she was feeling but because she knew where all this was headed.

Brian untied her bathrobe. He kept kissing her, pushed

her down against the bed, and she worried, briefly, that her still-damp hair was staining her parents' silk pillows.

"I have condoms," Brian whispered.

"That's, um, nice," Junie whispered back.

They had done it for the first and only time three weeks ago, before the rains came, on a Saturday in March when her mother was in Athens and her father was in Cleveland. They'd spent that morning tossing a Frisbee in Prospect Park and then ordered pizza and watched *Freddy vs. Jason* in the den Junie's mother had redecorated during the last full month she was in town. They'd started making out halfway through the movie—which wasn't that scary, wasn't even that funny—and pretty soon all their clothes were in a pile by the fireplace, a tangle of cords, T-shirts, underwear, and Birkenstocks. They'd been talking about having sex for months, Brian wheedling, Junie hedging; now, it seemed, it was finally time to get the thing over with.

She had tried not to watch as Brian fumbled with the condom. Instead she turned to the television, where Freddy Krueger was chasing the girl from Destiny's Child. In her head she heard the warning of her old Irish nanny, Mrs. Finnegan: *A lady's only as pretty as her virtue, lass. Love is sweet to drink but bitter to pay for.*

"I love you, Junie," Brian whispered.

She took a deep breath. "I love you too." Mrs. Finnegan's careful warnings dissolved in the pizza-scented air.

And so they did it. The pain was burning, stabbing, excruciating. She tried to block it out by staring at the family photos on the wall, but perversely, they only intensified the pain, for she could imagine each member of her half-Chinese, half-Jewish, all-judgmental family staring down at her in disgust. There was her short Jewish father, with the belly and the bald spot, her Chinese mother, all polish and sparkle, her grandma Wong, tiny and domineering, and her grandma Goldstein, stout and nearsighted like her dad. And right in the middle, Mrs. Finnegan, as much a member of the family as the rest of them, holding a six-year-old Junie on her lap. Was it Junie's imagination, or did the photo actually turn its head in shame? *A lady's only as pretty as her virtue, lass. What are you doing down there on the floor?*

Junie shuddered and looked at the television, where Freddy Krueger was brandishing his fingernails.

A minute later it was over. Brian rolled off her. "Oh my God," he muttered. "That was so totally great." Junie kept quiet. "Was it okay for you?" he asked, turning on his side, pushing the hair out of her face. His cheeks and the tips of his ears burned bright pink. He'd never done it before either.

"Sure," she said, doing her best to ignore the ache between her legs. "It was really nice."

"Yeah," Brian said dreamily. They were both quiet for a moment, breathing hard. Junie hoped she wasn't bleeding. Brian peeled off the condom and wrapped it in a tissue. "So you want to try it again later?" he asked. "Maybe after we finish the movie? I have a whole box of these," he added, holding the wadded-up tissue aloft. "I'm sure I'd last longer if we did it again."

"Um, actually, it's kind of not—" But she looked at him,

his eyes so big, his cheeks so pink, his expression so happy and hopeful. How could she deflate him? "Let's see how it goes," she said. "Maybe we should wait till tomorrow instead."

But the next day she stayed in bed. Her stomach was killing her, and she was exhausted. Brian left three messages on her machine; she sent him a page saying she had some kind of virus and was too wiped to even talk on the phone. He showed up at her house that evening with takeout chicken soup.

"Thanks," Junie said, but her stomach was still tied in knots, and she didn't much feel like eating. She kissed him good-bye on the front steps and stashed the chicken soup in the empty fridge.

In the days and weeks that followed, Brian remained affectionate, almost slobbery. He stuffed roses in her locker, kissed her passionately in the halls, practically started humping her in precalc that day they'd had a sub.

"I don't know what's going on with him," Junie marveled on the phone with her best friend, Celia. "Almost a whole year together and I've never seen him act like this."

"He's horny, Junie," Celia said, with her customary air of expertise. "He's like a happy, horny puppy dog. And he loves you. Enjoy all the attention if you can."

So Junie tried to enjoy it, but secretly, helplessly, she couldn't help but grow irritated. The more Brian salivated, the more she felt herself pulling away, but if he noticed, he kept quiet about it. Neither one of them wanted to mention the distance that was percolating between them. Junie wouldn't admit it to anyone—not her mother, not even to Celia—but Brian, the love of her life, with the tattoos and the thread necklaces and the shaggy hair and the faint grasp of Hindi, was starting, ever so slightly, to gross her out.

And then the rain began to fall.

"The condoms are in my bag," Brian said as they rolled around on her parents' burgundy comforter.

"Then they're probably soaked," Junie said.

"Nah, they're in foil packets. Waterproof."

"Oh." She knew she should just come out and say it, that she couldn't bear going through the whole sex thing again, that she just wasn't ready for it, that it hurt too much, made her feel too awkward. But for some reason she couldn't bring herself to open her mouth. She drew her knees up to her chest and looked pleadingly at Brian, hoping he'd guess the truth without her having to say it. "You know, I really think it'd be better to do our precalc homework. We've got that test Friday."

"You'd rather do precalculus than have sex?"

"It's just . . ." Junie hated the weakness in her voice. "We've got that test." She covered her mouth to suppress a cough; Junie sometimes burst into spontaneous coughing fits when she was nervous.

Brian was quiet for a second. Then he said, "Junie, what's going on?"

"Excuse me?"

"You realize you've been kind of cold lately, don't you?"

"Cold?" Junie repeated. Oh no. She wrapped her arms tighter around her knees.

"Icy. Like you're mad at me, except that I have no idea what I could possibly have done." Brian shook his head, sat up. "And this is the first time we've made out in weeks. So what's up?"

"Nothing, it's nothing." Junie sat up too. "You haven't done anything. I'm not mad at you. It's just, I mean . . ." She grabbed the bathrobe and pulled it on, tying it tight across the waist. "Between the weather and everything, I've just been a bit down. Seasonal affective disorder, you know?"

"But that only happens in the winter," Brian said. "It's April."

"Yeah, but it's been so rainy out."

Brian looked at Junie—well, it seemed at first like he was looking at her, but really he was trying to look right into her to see if there was anything inside that would give him some answers. But he didn't seem to see a thing. "You don't want to talk about it?" he said.

Junie paused. "I swear, Brian, there's nothing to talk about."

He nodded, found his boxers with his toe. Then he said, "The rest of my clothes are probably dry."

"What?"

"The rest of my clothes. Downstairs. They're probably dry now."

And for the next few uncomfortable minutes they busied themselves collecting Brian's shorts and shirt from the dryer and gathering his still-sodden messenger bag from upstairs.

10

"Listen," Junie said as she walked him to the front door. "It's so quiet."

"So?"

"So maybe the rain's slowing down."

Brian's expression was blank, empty, ominous. "Maybe it is," he said quietly.

Then he turned and left.

Sanskrit, Shakespeare, and Chili Sauce

In Brooklyn's emerging African American sculpture scene, Maximillian Clarke was developing a strong reputation for creations welded out of burnt-looking pieces of steel. Celia Clarke liked her father's work okay, but she wished he'd relax a little bit, allow something less aggressive into his artwork. Their living room, for example, looked like some violent gang's clubhouse: Max's spears and arrows hung from the walls, dangled from the ceiling, and lay scattered across the floor. Instead of a television or a couch the room featured three low benches surrounding a sculpture that Max called *Dying Pig*.

Celia's mother had died fourteen years ago, and ever since, Max had cast spears and spikes and brilliantly blunt objects. But as much as his sculpture was belligerent, Max Clarke himself was gentle and caring, and Celia just adored him.

"You studying at home tonight? I left some chili in the

fridge." Max was working at his studio in Red Hook, finishing up some projects for a new show. He called every day around five.

"Don't worry about me, Dad," Celia said, doodling on the front page of the previous day's *New York Times*, the phone crunched between her shoulder and her ear. "Danielle from my English class is coming over to work on a Shakespeare assignment; maybe we'll order from Peking Dragon."

"I'm glad you have company," Max said. "I like it better when you're not by yourself." Like all warriors, Celia's father had a protective streak.

"Daddy, you know I'll be fine."

"I know you will. Don't order in. Finish the chili so it doesn't go bad."

"You got it," Celia said, and hung up. It was five-fifteen and Danielle Battaglia wasn't due until six. Celia had just gotten home from teaching gymnastics, and she had forty-five minutes to get ready. But first she had to clean up the kitchen, light seven lavender candles, maneuver herself into the baddha konasana pose (back against wall, heels pressed together, backs of her hands resting gently on her knees), and meditate. This was a habit she'd grown to depend on during the past several months, and if she missed her daily meditation, she knew she'd get grumpy. Celia kicked off her stilettos, lit the seven candles, and dimmed the lights. Then she arranged herself on the living room floor, opposite one of her father's spears.

"Atha yoga anushasanam," she began, breathing deeply. *"Yogash chitta vritti nirodah. Tada drashtuh svarupe avasthanam.*

Vritti sarupyam itaratra." This was the only Sanskrit she knew.

"May the healing forces of the world come together to bring comfort, faith, and hope," she whispered to herself, letting the scent of lavender fill her nose. "May I bring the gifts of love and joy to everyone I come in contact with every day. May I be a provider of grace, truth, and generosity. May the unifying goodness of"—and here the doorbell buzzed loudly, jolting Celia out of her meditative trance. She checked her watch. Five thirty-two. Danielle had no business being this early.

"May the unifying goodness of—" The doorbell buzzed again. Celia leaned her head back against the wall, breathing in and counting to five. It was no good. The spirit was gone. "You were supposed to come at six!" she yelled at the ceiling. The doorbell buzzed one more time.

Celia got up, blew out her candles, and calmly went over to the intercom in the kitchen. She refused to be rushed. "You're early," she said into the button.

"Cee, it's me, I need to talk about Brian, please let me in. . . ." It was Junie, her best friend since they'd met trick-or-treating on Halloween twelve years ago, waiting in line for Reese's peanut butter cups at the same town house on DeGraw.

"What's going on, girl? Come on up." Celia buzzed her in and then relit the candles. Her best friend was panicked. It sounded like she could use a bit of the soothing power of lavender and maybe a few words of healing Sanskrit, too.

Fifteen minutes later the two girls were huddled over earthenware mugs in Celia's living room, Junie sniffling, Celia dripping honey into her friend's tea. "He looked like a statue when he left, Cee. And then he didn't kiss me good-bye. He *always* kisses me good-bye."

"Well, hell hath no fury like a man scorned, or something like that," Celia said. "What I don't get is why you don't just tell him that you're not ready to have sex again."

Junie sighed heavily, rested her head in her hands. "I don't know, I just can't. He won't understand. I mean, I already did it once, right? So why should I get all virtuous now? It makes no sense."

"Jesus, girl, just tell him the truth."

Junie shrugged and looked down at her tea. Celia noticed that she had taken off the turquoise bracelet Brian had given her. She was about to ask her why she'd removed it when the doorbell buzzed again. Junie looked up, startled.

"Danielle Battaglia, from my English class," Celia said. "We're supposed to work on *Much Ado About Nothing.*"

"Do you want me to leave?"

"Don't you dare." Celia buzzed Danielle up and then stood by the front door to wait for her, wrapped in a pink-and-silver silk kimono, her afro bedecked with tiny gold beads. This was how Celia dressed on casual days. In her stilettos she was almost six feet tall.

Two minutes later a wispy girl walked in, carrying a drippy umbrella. "Hey!" she said brightly. "Can you believe the rain out there?" She wore frosted pink lipstick and a gold-plate necklace studded with diamonds that spelled out her name. Celia went to school with a lot of girls who looked like this, girls who believed that gold jewelry and high ponytails were the height of fashion, girls who smoked Newports after school and had boyfriends named Damon and Vinnie. Mafia princesses, everyone called them, even the O'Donnell and Mikowski girls, who clearly had nothing to do with the mob.

"Danielle, this is Junie, my best friend. She lives down the street. Junie, this is Danielle."

"Nice to meet you."

"How you doing?" Danielle said, although she seemed to have no interest in Junie; she was staring wide-eyed at the landscape of Celia's living room.

"Man," Danielle said. "What's all this stuff supposed to be?"

"It's my father's sculpture," Celia said. "It's inspired by the tribal and aboriginal art of suffering indigenous populations worldwide."

"So what's this one supposed to look like?" Danielle asked, pointing to the sculpture in the middle of the floor.

"Oh, that." Celia sighed. "He calls that *Dying Pig*, but I think it actually symbolizes—"

"A dying pig," Danielle said, clearly bemused. "How weird. Who wants to come home and see a dying pig where the TV should be?"

Celia would tolerate no criticism of her father's luminous work. She rolled her eyes at Junie. "Danielle," she said, "would you like some tea?"

The girls reassembled themselves at the kitchen table, holding earthenware mugs and inhaling the scent of Meyer lemon and honey. Celia's kitchen was decorated with bright murals of flowers she had painted in junior high, and it felt much more cheerful than the living room.

"See, this is the kind of art I'm more usually drawn to, you know?" Danielle said, gesturing with her mug to the mural on the wall opposite the table. "Like where you can figure out what everything is."

"I understand," Celia said with an almost-hidden hint of condescension.

Junie rubbed her left wrist, where Brian's bracelet used to be. She'd taken it off before she left the house; for some reason wearing it made her feel guilty and stupid. He'd given it to her on their six-month anniversary, and she'd promised never to take it off. The bracelet was a symbol of how much they loved and trusted each other, but now it felt false, like how dare she wear his bracelet when she couldn't even have an honest conversation with him?

"Stop thinking about it," Celia said, noticing the look in Junie's eyes. "You're gonna drive yourself crazy."

"Something happen?" Danielle asked.

"Oh, well . . . my boyfriend. We had this totally weird afternoon and I'm still freaking out. . . ." Junie trailed off, unsure of how much she wanted to tell a stranger. "I've sort of been acting like a complete jerk lately, and today it blew up in my face," she summarized.

"Why have you been acting like a jerk?" Danielle asked. "You trying to dump him?"

"Oh my God, no!"

"'Cause I know some girls who do that. They don't want to be the bad guys, so they won't do the actual breaking up, but instead they just act like total bitches until the guy finally dumps them instead. You know Tonya Marino from our art class?" Danielle asked, raising a conspiratorial eyebrow at Celia. "She does that all the time."

"I'm not trying to break up with Brian," Junie said curtly. "It's just that we're having some issues right now."

"He wants to have sex and she doesn't," Celia clarified, and Junie shot her a dirty look.

"Well, why don't you want to do it?"

"It's a long story." She stirred her spoon around in her mug. This was really none of Danielle's business. "I sort of don't feel like talking about it anymore."

"So you're an avoider," Danielle said. "My mother's the same way."

"I'm a what?" Junie looked up, trying to figure out if she should be offended.

"An avoider." Danielle sipped her tea. "You have a non-confrontational personality and therefore you do whatever you can to avoid conflict. So instead of talking to your boyfriend about what's on your mind and risk having a fight, you feel safer pushing him away." Danielle faced down Celia and Junie's curious looks. "What? I read a lot of self-help."

"I've never thought of myself as an avoider."

"It's true that you go out of your way not to fight," Celia said. "You always have, ever since we were little."

"Don't worry," Danielle added. "It's not such a bad thing. Sometimes I wish I were like that too. I'm always picking fights, and it totally gets me in trouble. I can't keep my mouth shut ever."

"What do you mean?" Celia said.

"Dude, I almost got expelled last year for mouthing off to Sister Frances about not taking some part in the school musical. And I also almost got expelled freshman year for insubordination in gym class. I had my period and Sister Claudia still wanted me to play dodgeball!"

"Wow," Junie said.

"Oh yeah, and then I almost got expelled again for fighting with Angela Forenza in the halls last February."

"I remember that," Celia asked. "Everybody was talking about it the next day. What happened with you two, anyway?"

"It's this whole story," Danielle said. Instead of explaining herself, she scratched her knee for a second and turned to Junie. "Where do you go, anyway?"

"Brooklyn Prep," Junie said. "Down by the Verrazano."

"Yeah, I know that school," Danielle said. "I wanted to go there but, you know, my mom thought it was too expensive. Besides, she believes in Catholic schools. Nuns and everything. She thinks the nuns keep me out of trouble."

"Do they?" Junie asked.

"What do you think?"

"I think no," Junie said, after a minute.

"I almost got expelled three times in three years," Danielle said. "So I think you're right." She began to giggle, and then Junie joined in, tentatively. For some reason the giggles soon turned into a full stream of laughter, the way giggles sometimes will when nobody bothers to stop them; soon Celia couldn't help but join in. In a few minutes the three were doubled over, snorting and laughing with their mouths wide open. When the laughter finally tapered into hiccups, all three girls realized at once that they were starving.

Max had left only a small bowl of chili, not nearly enough for three hungry girls at 7 P.M. on a school night. So they pored through the kitchen cabinets to find something else to eat, dug into the fridge like archaeologists, but turned up little more than old tubes of tomato paste and cans of whipped cream.

"What the hell is this?" Danielle asked, opening a squat silver jar. She took a whiff and wrinkled her nose.

"Herring, probably," Celia said. "Pickled herring in cream sauce. My father loves to schmooze with the guy at the Jewish deli on Fourth Street, and he always comes home with samples."

"Weird. Don't you guys have any marinara sauce or anything?"

"Maybe we could cook these," Junie said, extracting a package of chicken legs from the bottom of Celia's pullout freezer. "We could have chicken legs in chili sauce."

"Or here's some teriyaki," Celia said, taking a jar out of the pantry. "It's never even been opened."

"Teriyaki chicken, yum."

"With chili," Junie said.

"And here's some garlic—do you guys like garlic bread?" Danielle asked. "I make really good garlic bread—it's one of those things I learned growing up."

"You know how to cook?"

"Oh yeah. Grew up with three Italian ladies, so of

course." Danielle put the garlic to her nose. "Good," she said. "It's still fresh."

The girls got to work, spreading out in every available corner of Celia's kitchen. She and Max lived in a large apartment on the top floor of a four-story building in Carroll Gardens. The apartment had been renovated twice in the twelve years they'd been there, and so the floors were smooth parquet, the ceilings were high and airy, and the bathrooms featured granite tiles and fancy brass metalwork. Nevertheless, the kitchen was still pretty small, and the girls bumped elbows with each other as they chopped garlic, reheated chili, and doused the chicken legs in teriyaki sauce.

"You got any bread for me?"

"Just this," Celia said, handing over half a stale baguette.

Danielle sighed and shook her head and then began spreading her garlic-butter mixture on the baguette. "Do me a favor and preheat that oven. We're gonna have to toast this thing good to soften it up."

Soon the kitchen was sweltering and the air was filled with the pungent smells of chili, teriyaki, and garlic. Celia handed out thick paper plates and plastic forks. "I don't feel like doing the dishes tonight."

They ate in the dining room off the kitchen, sitting on bamboo chairs at one end of the long teak table, over which swung a chandelier Max had welded out of discarded metal spoons. "You know, this bread really isn't bad," Celia said thoughtfully as she polished off her third piece.

"You know what it is?" Junie said. "The baguette is denser, so you get more garlic butter and less chewy bread."

She was glad to have her pre-fight-with-Brian appetite back. It was good to be around other girls, around friends.

"Hey," she said tentatively. "I mean, I don't know how you guys would feel about trying this again sometime, maybe with like actual recipes or something. But it might be fun to try cooking again. We could do it at my house if you wanted. My parents are never home."

"That'd be awesome," Danielle said. "I love to cook, but my grandmother's always in the way."

Celia, who ordinarily preferred not to socialize with other St. Margaret's girls, tapped her finger on her chin. *Please don't snob out,* Junie silently pleaded. *Don't make me look like an idiot.* "I could find recipes in my dad's old cookbooks," she finally said, and Junie sighed with relief.

"So you want to say Friday, then?"

"Great," Danielle said.

"Sounds good." Celia nodded.

Junie crunched on her garlic bread, full of optimism. This could be really fun. And anyway, it was good to have a plan that didn't rely on condoms, frank discussions, or sunny weather.

Coffee and Ginger

Danielle Battaglia lived on Fourth Place in Carroll Gardens, in an old wooden four-story house. The house belonged to three generations of women in her family; all were raised in Brooklyn, and none had any intention of leaving. Nonna, Danielle's grandmother, was born in an upstairs bedroom three weeks after her parents made the journey to New York from Sicily. Nonna had married Arturo Bollino in the downstairs parlor, celebrated the christenings of her children in the cheery backyard with the mulberry tree, and mourned her son and then her husband in the large front living room after they were killed by a sniper in Vietnam and a heart attack, respectively.

Danielle's mother, Rita, and Danielle's sister, Christina, both worked as lingerie saleswomen at Macy's and commuted together every morning on the F train. Rita and Christina looked alike, each short and roundish with enormous bosoms and wavy black hair. They both favored simple blouses and sensible shoes, and they both wore large gold crosses around their necks. Sometimes one or the other would make some remark about Danielle joining them at Macy's as soon as she graduated from high school, and Danielle would feel herself start to wilt.

Danielle's father left the family when she was four years old, running off to California with a woman whose name her mother still refused to mention. Danielle didn't know much about him; Christina said he'd been kind of a goofball and remembered him sneaking into her room with bowls of ice cream late at night. Christina also remembered him coaching her whiffleball team and taking her bowling at the Court Street Lanes after church on Sundays. Danielle used to be jealous that Christina had all those memories of their father. Christina was eight when he left, after all, and eight was old enough to remember things. But as she grew up, Danielle realized that she had something even better than bowling to remember her father by. Danielle was lucky enough to have inherited her father's face.

"It's not just that she's impossible," Danielle overheard her mother once say on the phone years and years ago. "It's that she looks just like Tom, and every day I have to see that jerk's smile. And I remember all that humiliation he put me through, and I just want to scream." Danielle had retreated into her bedroom, secretly pleased.

Each morning before school Danielle spent fifteen minutes brushing out her gold hair, tracing black eyeliner around her bright green eyes, and running Mauve Crystal lipstick over her lips. None of the other women in her family had gold hair or green eyes. None of the others stood five-foot-five or fit into size-four jeans. None of them had such delicate hands or high cheekbones, and Danielle knew that she was blessed and felt that these blessings, these gifts from her father, were what was going to keep her out of Macy's. She was sure of it.

"Daniella! *Bambina!* You're gonna be late!" It was Wednesday morning, and Nonna was calling from downstairs in her powerful voice. Even though she was born here in Brooklyn, she still peppered her speech with Italian terms of endearment.

"I'm coming, Nonna, you don't have to scream." Danielle grabbed her backpack from the top of the staircase and darted down three rickety flights to the kitchen, singing Christina Aguilera's "Beautiful" to herself.

"Good morning, precious," Nonna said. She was waiting at the foot of the stairs dressed in her usual housecoat, her gray-brown hair wrapped around dozens of curlers, a cup of coffee in her heavy hands. "Ooh, I love hearing you sing that song, *cara*. Did you sleep okay?"

"Not enough," Danielle said, leaning down a few inches to kiss her grandmother on the cheek. "Stupid Shakespeare project I'm working on."

"Shakespeare," Nonna said dreamily. "I remember seeing *Much Ado About Nothing* with your grandfather in Central Park—"

"I know, Nonna. I'm gonna be late." Danielle poked her head into the kitchen, where her mother and her sister were bent over their coffee. "See you later, guys."

"Have a good day at school," they said in one voice. Then her mother blew a kiss in her direction. Danielle grabbed a semolina roll off the counter and bounded out the front door into the gray Brooklyn morning.

Junie's morning didn't go quite as smoothly as Danielle's. Brian had called last night around one, just as she was finally falling asleep, spread out across the middle of her parents' bed with Joni Mitchell playing softly on the stereo. She picked up the phone, half startled out of a dream.

"It's me," he'd said. "What happened today?"

"I have no idea," Junie said, so relieved to hear his voice. "I'm so sorry. I feel terrible, I really do; I don't know what's wrong with me. . . ."

"Look, let's get some coffee early," Brian said. "I don't think the rain has started up again yet." On mornings when they both arrived before classes started, they usually met for coffee by the Brooklyn Prep duck pond. "We'll work this all out."

"I know we will," Junie said. "Thanks for calling, Bri. I'll see you tomorrow." She fell asleep hugging the phone.

But the next morning she was stupidly nervous, trying to figure out the right thing to wear, as if Brian hadn't seen everything in her closet already, as if he'd care at all what she was wearing. Still, getting dressed was an act of will. She pulled on a black polo shirt and stared at herself critically; it was all wrong: too boring, too preppy. There was the T-shirt from Carlsbad Caverns, nicely faded and a little tight, but it smelled like sweat—Junie had worn it jogging Sunday morning. The brown ribbed tank? She looked over at her clock. Ten of seven. Really she should already be out the door.

Junie groaned out loud and slid the polo shirt over her head. Then she pulled on her gray Earl corduroys (she had three identical pairs), tied her hair into a ponytail, and dotted concealer over a budding zit on her nose. But just as she was heading out of the house, the phone rang. It was her mother, calling in between business meetings in Brussels. "Anything new?"

"Since yesterday?" Junie said. "Not really. But I've got to go—I'm running late."

"Just tell me one thing about your day today. I feel guilty that I'm not there."

Junie's mother was a lawyer who dealt with transatlantic agricultural litigation. She was in Europe more often than the States. "You're never here," Junie said. "And I'm really gonna be late if I don't get going."

"So then just tell me about the weather today," her mother said.

"Gray. Probably more rain. Didn't you check CNN?"

"I did," she confessed. Sue Wong-Goldstein was a weather junkie, unable to leave in the morning before she knew what the temperature was like in key cities around the world. She wanted, she explained, to keep up on the places where her loved ones lived: her mother in San Francisco, her daughter in Brooklyn, and her husband, a corporate management consultant who worked all over the country.

"So when are you leaving?" Junie asked.

"Saturday night. From here it's on to Paris, then Riga."

"Where's that again?"

"Latvia. It'll be freezing."

"I'll send you an e-mail," Junie said. "I've really got to go now, Mom. It's almost seven."

"Seven, right. So what time is it here, then? I can't even keep up anymore."

"One P.M., Mom. You're on your lunch break. I'll talk to you later."

"You're such a smartie," Junie's mom said. "Have a good day."

Junie wished she could tell her mother about the tension with Brian, but she knew Sue didn't have time. The time difference worked so that when Junie woke up, her mother was eating lunch, and when Junie was heading home from school, Sue was calling it a night. Anyway, Junie couldn't deal with starting to tell her mother about the whole Brian saga only to be interrupted by a meeting on, say, the nuances of fertilizer distribution in the European Union.

Eight after seven. Junie shook out her hair, slicked on some Chapstick, grabbed her knapsack, and headed out the door. School started at 8:05. If the subway was on her side, she'd only be two minutes late to meet Brian.

It was only after she'd found a seat on the N train that she realized she'd forgotten to put the turquoise bracelet back on her wrist.

Months before Junie had even been officially introduced to Brian Cooper, she'd longed to be his girlfriend. This was not a unique aspiration. Half the female population at Brooklyn Prep wanted to go out with Brian Cooper, the new kid from Vermont with the blond shaggy hair and the tattered thread necklaces resting just above the collars of his Phish T-shirts. Brian was one of those instantly popular guys. He joined the ultimate Frisbee team (of course) and also varsity soccer and lacrosse, wrote a funny, laconic column for the school paper, and sported a tattoo on his wrist of a tiny blue sparrow in a cage. The girls would gaze at the tattoo and wonder, quietly, about its meaning. They didn't even know about his other tattoo, the dancing bear on his lower back.

Junie finally met Brian accidentally-on-purpose in art history class, sitting next to him every day and dropping her books often enough so that he eventually had to wonder who the clumsy girl was on his left. She'd never been that bold about meeting a guy before, but they only shared this one class together; even though it was a little sitcom-ish, she couldn't think of another way to get him to notice her. So every so often she knocked her books on the floor, and every so often Brian Cooper picked them up.   •

"God," she'd said eventually. "You must think I'm such a klutz."

He grinned his sweet, lazy grin. "Junie Goldstein, I noticed you a long time ago. You don't have to keep beating up your books for me."

Junie had done her best to look affronted. "I have no idea what you're talking about."

Brian shrugged, but as the lights dimmed and the slide show presentation of Jean-Louis David's neoclassic portraiture began, she could feel him sneaking glances at her. Her heart beat fast.

When the lights came back on, Junie realized that her notebook was covered in doodles of the word *Brian*. She slammed it shut but could still feel his eyes on her. Gathering every last molecule of her courage, she turned around and said: "So when were you planning on going to the Met?"

"The Met?" Brian said. "Were we supposed to do that?"

"You know," Junie said, trying to stay nonchalant. "For the Impressionism assignment. The thing about Renoir and Monet. 'Cause I was planning on going on Saturday, and if you wanted to come, I . . ." She drifted off, aware that she was about three words away from making a total ass of herself.

"I could do that," Brian said slowly. "That assignment's due pretty soon, right?"

"In two weeks," Junie said.

"So yeah, let's go," Brian said. "Saturday. Meet me on the front steps of the museum at, I don't know, noon?"

"Sounds good," Junie said, using every last ounce of her will to keep cool.

"Good," Brian said. "See you then."

Even strong-willed Junie could only keep her cool for so long. As soon as class was over, she locked herself into the private bathroom near the guidance counselors' offices to text-message Celia, jumping up and down with excitement.

All that was almost a year ago. Brian was no longer the demigod of her art history class; in fact, it turned out that underneath his arctic-cool exterior was a charming sweetheart of a guy. There were so many things Junie never would have expected about him: that he knew the names of all the constellations, for instance, or that his favorite channel was BBC America, or that, after a trip to India the previous summer, he'd started trying to teach himself Hindi by watching endless Bollywood movies. But these were the idiosyncrasies Junie had fallen in love with. So now why was she pushing him away?

"Hey," he said quietly as Junie wiped off the damp bench and sat down by his side. The skies were still dark, but at least it wasn't raining again. She dropped her book bag on the grass as Brian handed her a latte from Starbucks. "Soy milk," he said.

"Thanks." She kissed him on the cheek.

They were both quiet for a minute, sipping their coffees, watching the geese chase each other around the pond.

"So what's been going on lately?" Brian finally said. "Why have you been acting like a stranger?"

"I don't know." Junie was instantly nervous and defensive. She had never felt this way around Brian before they had sex. "I guess I didn't realize how I'd been behaving."

"Come on. You've been completely stiff around me, you don't return my calls half the time, you *never* want to . . ." He trailed off and drummed his fingers on the top of his coffee cup. In the pond two mallards reared up in the water and beat their wings, competing over something invisible.

Junie knew that it was time to stop being an avoider. The only thing she could do was tell him honestly: that the sex had been painful and she felt profoundly guilty about it, that she didn't think she was ready for the kind of commitment having more sex seemed to imply. After all, he deserved the truth. And what was the worst thing he could say? Yet pathetically, absurdly, when she opened her mouth, all that came out was a feeble, "I'm sorry."

Brian watched the mallards as they continued to flap their wings.

Oh, this was insane. "Look, after we—"

"Are you interested in somebody else?"

She was so startled that all she could manage was a shabby denial: "Brian, no, are you crazy?"

" 'Cause if it's about someone else, the worst thing you could possibly do is not tell me. I'm not here to get used, Junie. For almost a year we've had a really good thing, but if you're into someone else, then you owe me the respect—"

"Brian, Jesus, stop. There's nobody else. I love you, come on. You know that." A crisp wind blew Junie's hair into her face. She felt her eyes start to water, but whether it was the wind or something else, she wasn't sure. She covered her mouth with her hand to stifle a nervous cough.

"You love me?" he asked, still staring at the pond.

"Of course," Junie said softly. She put her hand on his arm, but it felt stiff with resistance.

"Then why did you take off my bracelet?"

Oh God, no. Junie felt her heart plummet. "Why did I— your bracelet? I don't know, after yesterday I felt weird about wearing it, and then I meant to put it back on this morning, but I was running late, and I just forgot—Brian, does it really matter?"

He turned to her, but he wasn't listening. His cheeks were

red. He sipped his coffee. He looked like he was going to say something, and then he looked like he changed his mind. And then, shaking his head, he got off the bench and walked casually toward school.

"And you didn't talk to him for the rest of the day?" Celia asked.

"Not a word," Junie said. They were sitting at a corner table at the Smith Street Coffee Carriage, sunlight streaming through the large front windows and warming their hands. After almost two entire weeks of gloom the weather had gone from gray to brilliant in the space of a morning, and the girls luxuriated in it, tilting their chins up to the sun.

The Coffee Carriage was a Cobble Hill institution, full of cushy tattered sofas and scarred wooden tables. There was a carved bookcase full of chess and backgammon sets, a well-stocked magazine rack in the corner, and a tabby cat who slept in the window seat. Celia was supposed to meet Danielle here to finish their Shakespeare assignment; she liked the Coffee Carriage all right although as usual, she was the only black person in the place. Junie was keeping her company, picking dully at a cinnamon roll.

"I don't know what came over me," she said. "It was like I was some kind of deaf-mute. And then, when I finally *could* speak, everything I said came out wrong."

Celia made a sympathetic noise and patted Junie's hand.

"I just can't understand what's happened to me lately. Everything I thought I knew about myself seems off some-how. I thought I wanted to be with Brian. I thought I wanted to be in a relationship. But when it came time for me to fight for what I thought I wanted, I totally froze. It's like I can't even figure out my own heart."

"Maybe Brian's figured it out for you," Celia said, as gently as she possibly could. Junie looked at her quizzically, so she continued. "It's possible you're just ready to move on. I've been thinking about what Danielle said last night, and it makes sense. Maybe you're forcing Brian to break up with you because you don't have the nerve to break up with him."

"But why would I want to do that?"

"Well," Celia said, reaching out for her friend's hand, "it could be you're just one of those people who's used to being alone. I mean, let's face it, you spend a lot of time by yourself. You're either at home alone, or you're out in the park running, or you're downloading music for your iPod. You're like a lone wolf, Junie. So maybe that's why you're resisting this relationship. It's gotten too serious, and you're just not ready for that."

"But I don't want to be a lone wolf."

"I'm not sure," Celia said, "that you can help it." She picked a crumb from Junie's cinnamon roll. She and Junie were similar in so many ways: they were both only children, both loved to roam the streets of Brooklyn, and both looked a little out of the ordinary: pale, tiny Junie and too-tall Celia. Neither one had all that many friends besides each other. When Celia talked about lone wolves, she knew what she was talking about; she was a lone wolf herself. Junie was just about to comment on that fact when Danielle emerged out of nowhere.

"Hey, Celia. Oh, hi, Junie." She sat down right in between them. "Didn't go so good with the boyfriend, huh?"

"Excuse me?"

"Well, no offense, but you look like hell. Anybody want some coffee?"

"I look like hell?"

"I mean, just like you've been crying or something. Like somebody gave you some bad news. I'm gonna go get a cappuccino. You're sure you don't want any—" Danielle stood up, froze for a second, and then sat right back down.

"Oh my God, oh my God."

"What is it?" Celia said.

"Oh my God. Steve Reese. That bastard. Don't look."

"Who's Steve Reese?" Celia asked, leaning back so she could take a peek at the guy pouring coffee behind the counter. He had tattoos up and down both arms and dyed yellow hair and was wearing a stained T-shirt that said VIRGINIA IS FOR LOVERS. There was a teasing good humor in his smile, in the way he bantered with customers.

"I said *don't look*," Danielle said, hiding her face in her hands. "We used to date. Like three months ago. And then I caught him cheating on me and I haven't seen him since. . . . I can't believe he got a job at the Coffee Carriage of all places. He totally hates coffee." Danielle stared at the table, keeping her hands on either side of her temples to hide her face.

"He's cute," Celia said objectively.

"I *know*."

"I think he's looking at you," Celia said.

"Oh my God."

35

"Give me a break." Junie stood up, annoyed that Danielle was interrupting their conversation with all her drama. "I'm getting some coffee. Anybody need anything?"

Danielle looked up at Junie, wide-eyed with anxiety. "Could you just order me a cappuccino? Skim milk, extra foam? I'd go with you, but I'm . . . paralyzed."

Junie rolled her eyes again and marched off to give her order. Three minutes later she sat back down at their table. "Steve's bringing it over himself," she said.

"Oh my God," Danielle whispered as Steve Reese appeared with three espresso-based beverages on a tray. He was even cuter close up, Celia noticed, with dark brown eyes and full lips. Even though he was thin, firm muscles bulged under his T-shirt. He looked like he was at least twenty-one. "Were you gonna say hi or what?" he asked, plunking Danielle's cappuccino down in front of her.

"You seemed busy," Danielle said. She was picking at a cuticle, doing her best to seem blasé.

"That so?"

"How you been?" She looked up at him then.

"I've been fine." Steve took a seat. Junie and Celia might as well have disappeared.

Danielle coolly sipped her cappuccino. It was a remarkably unruffled performance, Celia considered. Danielle pushed her hair off her face and smiled, serene as the Mona Lisa. "And how's Angela?"

"Oh, you know," Steve said. He touched Danielle lightly on the arm. "I don't see her much anymore."

"You don't? That's too bad. I thought you two might

have really had something together. . . ." And suddenly Celia realized what Danielle's near-expulsion fight with Angela Forenza had been about. Steve and Angie must have gotten busy behind Danielle's back.

"You know what?" she said, standing. "Maybe you and I should just finish that Shakespeare thing later. I'll call you."

"You sure?" Danielle blinked. "I'm sorry, I just got—"

"Distracted, I know. It's fine," Celia said. Junie stood up too. "It was nice to meet you, Steve."

"Yeah, yeah, you too," he said, never taking his eyes off Danielle.

Back home, Celia changed out of her uniform into her after-school clothes: a velour tube top, velour pants, and a pair of gold Jimmy Choo sandals she'd bought secondhand at a vintage store in SoHo. Her bedroom had the tiniest closet, barely big enough to hold her shoe collection, so Celia filled the rest of her room with old dressers and bureaus, home to her vast collection of sweaters, jeans, skirts, and tees. She draped her bed with Indian fabric, hung Chinese lanterns from the ceiling, and laid an imitation-Persian rug on the floor. There was no desk in the room, however, so Celia usually did her homework in the kitchen.

It was five o'clock, almost time for meditation. Still, she thought she should probably finish her trigonometry problem set before attempting to clear her mind. She spread out the homework on the table, fished a pencil from her knapsack, turned the radio on to the jazz station, and got down to business. Question one: At an altitude of ten kilometers, how far from the airport should an airplane begin its descent if safety regulations require that it descend at a three-degree angle? Okay, a problem like this required a tangent ratio, so Celia got out her calculator and was immediately interrupted by her father's hearty hello.

"Dad?" Celia turned around. "Why are you home so early?"

"Happy to see me?" he asked, bending down to kiss her head. Max was a huge man, six and a half feet tall and broad as a linebacker, but in his work uniform of greasy green pants and a white smock he looked about as imposing as one of Santa's elves. It helped that he had such a sweet smile.

"Cee, I want you to meet someone," Max said, gesturing to a person half hidden in the hallway. A woman in a neat black suit emerged, holding a tiny fluffy dog. "This is Jane Hayworth. Remember, I told you about her? She owns the gallery where I'm showing next month."

"Nice to meet you," Celia said, standing and reaching out to shake Jane's hand. She had a strong grip for a little woman. "Cute dog."

"This is my Ginger," Jane said in a British accent, holding up the dog's paw and waving it. "Ginger just *loves* your father's artwork. Ginger is so *excited* about the upcoming show, aren't you, my little darling angel?" Jane buried her head in the dog's neck and made a farting noise with her lips.

"That's—that's really great." Celia glanced up at her father to share a disparaging look, but to her surprise, Max was gazing fondly at Jane.

"We've just been at the studio, making selections for the

gallery," he said. "Jane had never been to Red Hook before. She didn't know anything about it."

"Did you like it?" Celia asked, wondering how Jane could manage on Red Hook's pitted sidewalks in her pointy high heels.

"Oh, I loved it," Jane exclaimed. "Loved it! The views! The space! The old docks and factories! It felt so terribly avant-garde, very Shoreditch in the nineties, you know what I mean?"

"I'm not sure I do."

"Shoreditch is a part of London, Cee," Max explained, scratching Jane's dog on the head.

"Back in the nineties it was very *branché*, very dangerous."

"*Branché?*" Celia repeated, taking a step backward.

"*Branché*, darling. French for hip, brilliant, exciting, *nouveau*. Just like your fabulous sandals."

Jane flashed a huge smile. "Max, why don't you show me the rest of the apartment? I'm just dying to see what you keep in your little Brooklyn hideaway." The dog yapped. "Don't you want to see the rest of Max's sculpture, Ginger? Oh, I *know* you do, my little angel girl."

As soon as they abandoned the kitchen for the living room, Celia poured herself a glass of water to keep from gagging.

An hour later Jane was gone and Max was in the kitchen, humming as he sautéed chicken breasts. Celia pretended to ignore him and concentrated on her problem set. Her father didn't sing a lot, but when he did, it usually signaled that he was in an unconscionably good mood.

"So what'd you think?" he asked, slinging capers into the frying pan. "She's something, isn't she?"

"Oh, she seemed like something," Celia said. She turned her rickety wooden chair around and watched Max squeeze lemon onto the chicken. It was chicken picatta night at the Clarke house, probably over a bed of linguine. The small, bright kitchen smelled like garlic. Max *was* in a good mood.

"She's from London, you know. Only she's been living here for the past three years, trying to make some headway in the gallery scene. Remember that Nigerian show? With the tiger blood? That was hers."

"I don't remember."

"It was pretty renegade stuff, especially for the Upper East Side. But of course in London they're doing bisected cows stuffed in vats of formaldehyde. A little tiger blood's nothing for a gallery owner from London."

"Sounds like quite a woman, Dad."

"Yeah," Max said dreamily, slicing scallions into the pan. "You want this extra crispy or just regular?"

"What is this, KFC?" Celia got up to set the table. "Regular will be fine."

"The thing about her"—Max plunged linguine into a pot of boiling water—"is that she's so little, but she's so tough. You see her carrying around that dog and you think she's some kind of lightweight, but then she starts talking about art and you realize that this woman knows her stuff."

"Dad, you're too susceptible to flattery."

"Perhaps," Max said. "Get out the colander, will you?"

Celia put the colander in the sink and set the kitchen

table with the bright red Fiestaware her father had let her pick out years ago, when she decided that they needed matching dishes in the house. (Max had been content to eat off cracked Salvation Army china, which he thought had character.) She set out the dark linen napkins and the blue glass goblets for the ginger beer they drank with most meals.

"Anyway, she's kind of cute, isn't she?" Max asked in a strained-casual voice as he drained the linguine.

Celia almost dropped her fork. "You've got to be kidding me."

Max placidly tossed the noodles.

"Well," Celia said, trying to strike a diplomatic note. "I guess she's okay, if your taste runs to tiny white women."

The two of them sat down across from each other and Max poured them each some ginger beer. "I wonder if she likes me," he said.

Celia knew that she should be indulgent. "She'd be a fool not to, Dad."

"Ah, Cee," Max said, reaching across the table to cuff her gently on the chin. "You're much too kind."

"I am not."

"Are too."

Celia didn't tell him that he had a big piece of green scallion wedged between his two front teeth.

At a quarter to midnight Danielle sat up and buttoned her school vest over her stretch lace T-shirt. Part of her couldn't believe that she was back in Steve Reese's crap-filled bedroom, and part of her felt like she'd never left.

"Where you going?" Steve asked, reaching up to rub her arm. They had been here since eight, when Steve's shift at the Coffee Carriage finally finished. They'd ordered Chinese food, listened to the new demo of his band, and, after lots of smooching on his slightly gritty futon, had sex for the first time in many months. Even though she knew she should feel ambivalent about being here again, Danielle was fairly blissed out. A torn condom wrapper was stuck to her leg.

"I've got to get home," she explained sadly. "Curfew."

"Forget your curfew," Steve said. "Spend the night."

"Man, don't I wish," Danielle said. Steve looked so beautiful lying there on his futon, his hands resting lazily above his head. His arms were decorated with tattoos of the Chinese symbols for loyalty, justice, and honor; he had a peace symbol inked below his belly button and an anarchy symbol on the back of his thigh, a few inches below his butt.

"So why don't you stay, then?" he asked.

"Don't be an idiot." Danielle looked around the room one more time. It really was just as she remembered it, a crappy room in a crappy apartment on Bergen Street, clothes strewn about and no sheets on the futon and shiny bootleg CDs littering the floor like so much snowfall. Steve's bass guitar was propped up in the corner, balanced on a hardback copy of the collected works of Charles Bukowski.

"When will I see you again?"

"Whenever you want," Danielle said, leaning down for a kiss. Steve's breath smelled like General Tso's chicken.

"I want to see you soon."

"Good."

"Like tomorrow."

"Good," Danielle said, kissing him again. Then she took her backpack from the floor and tiptoed out of his bedroom and the apartment he shared with two roommates: Derek, a tattoo artist, and Shrub, who sang in his band. As she was sneaking out, Shrub stuck his head out his bedroom door, letting a cloud of marijuana smoke escape. "Danielle Battaglia!" he said. "It's nice to have you back!"

"It's nice to be back, Shrub." Danielle grinned.

Walking the eight blocks back to her house, Danielle collected her thoughts. Was she happy she had reconnected with Steve? Well, truth be told, yes and no. Steve was totally hot, funnier and smarter and cooler than any of the high school boys she sometimes came in contact with. He knew how to kiss her so that her lips actually tingled, and when they had sex, he could get a condom on without screwing it up. (Danielle had only had sex with one other guy, messing around after a cousin's wedding, but he was a total spaz, so nervous he couldn't even unroll the condom without his hands shaking.)

When Danielle was with Steve, she felt glamorous, sexy—even special. Steve had a way of concentrating on her that made her feel like she was the only girl in the world worth paying any attention to at all. Once he'd even written a song about her, just him and a guitar; the song was called "Good Danielle," which was kind of corny, but nobody had ever written a song about her before or even a lyric.

But on the other hand, she knew he was a creep. Back in January they had dated for a few weeks, and she felt incredible the whole time, breaking her curfew and risking Nonna's righteous lectures just to spend an extra few hours in his arms. She'd listened to his band practice over and over, acted interested in the things his stupid friends had to say, and even had sex with him when she would rather have just sat around talking. And then one Sunday afternoon she showed up unannounced, simply meaning to surprise him. He'd left the door open like the chump he was and all she'd had to do was peek in to see what in the back of her mind she'd always suspected she might see: Angela Forenza, the biggest slut at St. Margaret's, totally naked on top of Steve. Up and down they went, moaning and sighing and laughing all at once. Something about it was transfixing. Danielle watched for thirty seconds at least before screaming, "Fuck you!" into Steve's bedroom and turning around and racing for home.

That was months ago, but the memory of it remained humiliating.

Still, was it possible Steve had changed?

The house on Fourth Place was asleep, thank God, when Danielle walked through the front door. She could even hear Nonna snoring through the walls of her first-floor bedroom. Danielle took off her shoes and snuck up the stairs, past her mother's room, past her sister's, and finally to her own at the end of the hall. It smelled like the gardenia candles her mother brought home from Macy's. The carpeting was fluffy and pink. It was clean, feminine, and orderly, the exact opposite of Steve's.

Tagliatelle, Tiramisu, and the Number Seven Special

In the thirty-two hours since Brian stopped talking to her, Junie had run sixteen miles. Coach praised her on her discipline, but discipline had nothing to do with it: Junie was running away from heartbreak as fast as she could, finishing the single-K sprints half a minute before her teammates, tackling mile drills like she was training for the nationals.

"You keep going like that, you'll hurt your knees," Amanda Begosian whispered during warm-ups, sets of thirty lunges on the soft soccer-field grass. Amanda was Junie's chem lab partner and one of the best runners on the team, but she'd had knee surgery the year before and was paranoid about injury.

"I'll be okay," Junie said as the girls flipped onto their backs for crunches. "I'm just pushing to improve my time."

"Hey, what's the deal with you and Brian?"

Great. Did the whole world already know? Amanda Begosian could spread gossip like wind spreading fire. Even worse, Junie had always suspected her of having a minor crush on Brian. "What do you mean?" Junie asked, playing dumb.

"Dan Cho told me," Amanda said. She wiped the sweat beads from her upper lip. "He said you guys had a fight because you've got a crush on a guy from another school. Of course I told him that you would *never* cheat on—"

"Amanda, that's total crap," Junie said, curling up to her knees. "Tell Dan he has no idea what he's talking about."

"I told him already that it didn't sound true to me either. But Dan said that Brian confronted you about it, and you told him you needed time to make up your mind, which is why—"

"I don't even want to know." Junie held her breath to keep from cursing in frustration. She pulled herself up into another crunch, inhaled, exhaled, curled back down.

"I'm just telling you what I've been hearing." Amanda's face was now completely drenched, sweat pouring down from her hairline and pooling in the wells of her collarbone. She had always been a heavy-sweating kind of girl, and nobody liked to get too close to her after long runs on hot days.

"Fine, but I'd appreciate it if you didn't repeat it. It's not true, and it's . . . it's hurtful."

"Oh, get over yourself, Junie. You don't have to be so totally uptight—"

"What exactly do you mean by uptight?"

But then, much to Junie's relief, Coach blew a fierce whistle at them, a signal to shut up and crunch.

Junie came home that night just as the skies were beginning to darken, picking up a Peking Palace broccoli number seven on the way. She dropped the takeout on the vast marble-topped kitchen table, trying not to notice how oppressively empty her house felt. Twenty years ago, when her parents bought the place, it was a slightly dilapidated building on a slightly dilapidated street that, according to real-estate rumor, was due to start gentrifying any second. Junie's parents hired architects, contractors, and interior designers, painstakingly renovating the town house into a temple of late-1980s swank. They lined the floors with Brazilian ebony, ordered wallpaper from Paris, bought rugs at an auction in Istanbul. The couches were leather, the counters were granite, and there was a Steinway in the formal sitting room, even though nobody in Junie's family knew how to play the piano.

And then they both got promoted to even higher positions, and the business trips began. First just a day at a time, and then a few days, and then, by the time Junie was ready for school, her parents were gone for weeks on end, scheduling trips so that on the day one of them came home, the other one was upstairs packing suitcases. The August before Junie was to start kindergarten, her mother placed a desperate ad in the *New York Times*. Mrs. Finnegan arrived on the first of that September, stout and gray haired, smelling like chocolate chip cookies.

"I'll be taking care of you now," she'd said to Junie in a thick Irish brogue, attempting to tickle her under the chin. Junie, terrified, hid behind her mother, who was busy checking the paper for the weather in Vienna.

But there was nothing to fear from Mrs. Finnegan, who

loved Junie almost as much as she loved her own daughters back in Ireland. It was Mrs. F. who took Junie to Girl Scout meetings, Mrs. F. who cheered her on at track, Mrs. F. who told her what to do the first time she got her period. (*"Put this here in your panties, and you might want to skip practice today."*) A disciplinarian and a stickler about grades, Mrs. Finnegan made sure Junie came home by eleven (even on weekends), finished her homework, and only watched half an hour of television every day.

But Mrs. Finnegan also had a slightly wilder side—she had a wicked sense of humor, for instance, and liked to tell naughty jokes. (*"What's an Amish woman's fantasy? Two Mennonite."*) She subscribed to British and Irish newspapers as well as the papers from Los Angeles and Washington, D.C., just so that she'd have a broad sense of what was going on in the world. She loved Harrison Ford movies, especially ones where he played a cop. And she spent her vacations with her daughters in Spain, where she ate dinner at midnight and learned to flamenco dance.

As Junie got older, she did her best not to notice that Mrs. Finnegan was getting older too. But last July, while she was preparing to leave for training camp, Mrs. Finnegan announced that after all this time in America, it was time to head back to Galway, where she came from. She was almost seventy-six years old, after all. Her arteries were starting to harden, and she had developed a tremor in her right hand. She wanted to be near her family again, her real family, her own daughters and grandchildren.

Dismayed, Junie's parents agreed that there was little chance of finding a competent replacement, and anyway,

Junie was practically seventeen and certainly capable of taking care of herself. They handed her an ATM card and a cell phone and assured her, and each other, that everything would be fine. Junie tried not to feel abandoned, but still, the loss stung and continued to sting. So now, alone in this giant spiffy town house, Junie often stared mournfully into Mrs. Finnegan's old bedroom. Mrs. F. lived with her younger daughter now; she needed someone to take care of her the way she'd taken care of Junie for all those years.

Poking at her congealing number seven special, Junie was overwhelmed by how much she missed Mrs. Finnegan. She could pick up the phone and call, but it was seven o'clock already, which meant it was midnight in Ireland, which was just too late to wake up an old lady. Before she left, Mrs. F. had promised to be there if Junie ever had an emergency. But was depression the same thing as an emergency?

Junie turned on the television, scrolling through the possibilities: *Simpsons* rerun, *TRL*, news, news, *Jeopardy!*, news. She clicked it off and took another poke at her takeout. Just then the phone rang, and Junie grabbed for the receiver so quickly she almost dropped it.

"Hey, girl." Celia, sounding like her usual self, cheerful and composed. Junie wasn't much for envying people, but right now she wished she could be Celia, with her dad at home and her lavender candles and her total lack of boy problems. "Just checking in about tomorrow."

"Tomorrow?"

"Remember, dinner with Danielle? You still want to do that?"

"Oh, right," Junie said. "I forgot. Yeah, let's still do it. Seven o'clock work for you?"

"Perfect. I'll tell Danielle."

Junie hung up the phone and took a bite of cold broccoli. Brian was ignoring her. Mrs. F. was in Ireland. Her parents were thousands of miles away, and she had just noticed a cramp developing in her lower-right quad. Perfect. She pushed the takeout away. Maybe a home-cooked dinner with the girls was exactly what she needed to cheer her sorry ass up.

The next day at school Junie did her best to avoid anyone who could bring her down—namely, Amanda Begosian and Brian. She sat with Rudy Jakes and Sara Kimble at lunch since they were too caught up in student council politics to care much about Brian-Junie gossip. She ate her sandwich listlessly and listened to chatter about a proposal to eliminate the vending machines in the front hallway. During track she ran as fast as she could, paying attention only to her legs, Coach, and the cool April wind on her face. And on the way home from practice she stopped at the Key Food just to ensure she had basic provisions on hand; her family cooked so rarely that she couldn't even be 100 percent certain there was salt and pepper in the house.

Freshly showered, Junie arranged her purchases on the cool countertop. Salt, pepper, garlic, onions, olive oil, eggs, and milk. The kitchen was a streamlined cooking machine: Sub-Zero fridge, Amana range, butcher-block island with a marble pastry wheel—yet there was no food in the fridge, no spices in the spice rack, and no chopping boards stacked up on the counters. It felt more like a stage set than a real room, and for some reason she found this state of affairs embarrassing. What would Danielle think?

Junie found a clean white apron hanging on a peg in the pantry and tied it around her waist. That felt official. She tied her hair back in a ponytail and wiped her hands on the apron and decided to sponge down the already neatly sponged countertops just to have something to do until Cee and Danielle arrived. The housekeeper had been there that day, vacuuming invisible particles of dust and swabbing shiny floors shinier still with Lysol. Nevertheless, this cooking idea had Junie feeling domestic, and so she scrubbed the countertops with vigor.

Danielle arrived first, bearing various parcels wrapped in white paper and tied up in string. "I went to my cousin's store in Manhattan after school," she said, unloading the parcels onto the granite countertop, making herself right at home. "He sells all kinds of stuff—chocolate and bread and pasta and whatever. But they're mostly famous for the cheese. They make their own mozzarella and ricotta. Piccolo Dairy on Sullivan, you know it?"

Junie shook her head, and Danielle looked disappointed. "Well, maybe it's just famous for Italian people, I don't know. My uncle started the place forty years ago, but now he's in semi-retirement and it's mostly my cousin who runs the shop these days. Rob, his whole world is cheese. It's really too bad he's such a dork, 'cause he's cute."

Danielle continued to unwrap her parcels. A shiny, dripping ball of mozzarella cheese, three tiny veal cutlets, thin and pinkish white, a box of fresh pappardelle, dusted in cornmeal and springy to the touch, and a perfect square of tiramisu. "My grandmother made that for us," Danielle said. "It's the best thing you're ever gonna eat in your entire life, I swear."

"I had no idea tiramisu was something a real person could make," Junie said, impressed. "I thought it was just something they invented for restaurants."

"Are you kidding?" Danielle laughed. "My grandmother hasn't eaten in a restaurant in probably twenty years." Danielle cleaned up the discarded strings and set the cutlets on a plate, and Junie marveled at her ease. She still felt slightly nervous around Danielle—slightly intimidated—but Danielle just seemed like herself, totally unperturbed. She sang softly as she patted the cutlets with paper towels.

The doorbell rang again, and Celia entered with an overstuffed grocery bag in each arm. They had enough food for an army.

"I couldn't find fresh oregano at the Key Food," she said. "They only had basil."

"We'll live," Danielle said. She was going through Junie's drawers, searching for knives. "Where do you keep your paring knives, Junie?"

"Total mystery." Junie didn't want to admit that she had no clue what a paring knife was. "You're welcome to look."

"Would anyone object if I turned on the stereo?" Celia asked, waving a small leather case in the air. "I brought my music with me."

"What do you got?"

"Oh, you know, the good stuff. Stevie Wonder, Marvin Gaye, a little Aretha . . ."

"That's the good stuff?" Danielle giggled. "Lite FM?"

"Get outta here. My taste is *classic*." Celia pressed play on the CD player built into the kitchen wall, and soon the room was flooded with the sweet sound of Aretha Franklin singing "Do Right Woman."

"Mmm . . ." Junie said. "I love this song." Junie's own musical preferences were highly adaptable; she loved to download music, but she usually just picked whatever her friends liked, and so half the time she was listening to Brian's mixes of Phish, the Dead, and the String Cheese Incident, and the other half of the time she was listening to Sam Cooke, Ray Charles, and Ike and Tina Turner with Cee.

"I guess it's not so terrible," Danielle said. "My mom listens to this stuff." She was washing the basil in the sink; casually, almost carelessly, she sang a few bars, as though she were in the shower or driving along a highway. Cee and Junie stopped putting away the groceries and stared.

"Danielle, you've got a beautiful voice!" Celia said.

"Oh, not really." She busied herself with the basil, avoiding Celia's dazzled expression.

"Why don't you sing in choir or something, Danielle? Sister Frances would totally love to have you."

"I don't know," Danielle said. "It's not really my thing. I never really liked what they sing in school choirs. It's not like I, you know, yearn to praise Christ in song."

"You could sing the secular stuff," Celia said, but Danielle just shrugged.

Junie fished a cast-iron skillet from a drawer underneath the counter and handed it to Danielle, who dashed in some olive oil and threw in a handful of chopped garlic. It was clear to Junie that she didn't want to talk about singing.

"Well, all I'm saying is that a voice like yours is an incredible gift," Celia said, pointing at the thin pink strip of veal. "What do you want me to do with this?"

Danielle ignored the compliment and took the veal from Celia's hands. "You should dredge it in the flour, like so," she said, running it through a low dish of flour that had been perked up with a shake of pepper. Then she laid the cutlet in the cast-iron pan, where it sizzled in the olive oil and released a gorgeously pungent smell. The veal turned white and then a pale golden color, and Danielle flipped it over. Celia attempted to dredge the next cutlet, holding the meat at its very edge like it was toxic.

"What are you afraid of?" Danielle asked. "It's just dinner."

"I know, but I've never—I mean I don't—" Celia plopped the veal into the bowl, releasing a mushroom cloud of flour. Her shiny red shirt turned white.

"You've got to be kidding me." Danielle picked the veal up and rolled it around in the bowl. "If you're gonna eat meat, you can't be afraid to touch it."

"But don't people usually wear gloves when they do this?"

Danielle laughed—and did Junie hear a bit of superiority in her laugh?—as she dredged the other cutlet and dropped it in the oil. "Can you flip these with a spatula or will that gross you out?"

"Give me that spatula," Celia said, "and don't be smart."

"And what about you?" Danielle turned her kitchen-queen act on Junie, who was trying to figure out how to drop the noodles into the boiling water without scalding herself. "Man, what are you doing? Here, use these," she said, handing Junie a pair of long-handled tongs.

"We have tongs?" Junie asked, using them to lower pappardelle into the pot.

"In that drawer over there. This place is like friggin' Williams-Sonoma. I can't believe you don't cook more with all this cool stuff you have."

Junie shrugged. "I'm busy."

"Everybody's busy," Danielle said. "But we've all got to eat, so you might as well cook." She lowered the flame under Junie's pot. "Anyway, now you just have to watch carefully," she instructed, "and take the noodles out as soon as the water starts to bubble up. It doesn't take very long with fresh pasta."

Fifteen minutes later the girls sat down to a table loaded with fresh mozzarella and arugula salad, pappardelle with tomatoes and basil, and the thin slices of veal, garlicky and browned on the edges. For a moment Junie wished Brian were here to join them. He loved Italian food.

"I can't even believe how good this smells," Celia said, twirling pasta around her fork.

"I know," Junie said. "The Wong-Goldstein house has not seen a dinner this fabulous since Thanksgiving."

"It's just basically how my grandmother cooks," Danielle said, taking a bite of her veal. "It's like a little bit of this and then a little of that and then she kicks in some salt and pepper and she's done."

"Maybe next time we could invite her to dinner," Junie said, loving the taste of pappardelle in her mouth. Celia had decided to compete with Danielle's mastery of all things kitchen, inventing a tomato sauce recipe. It was wonderful, helium light: nothing more than chopped hothouse tomatoes, a scattering of basil, sea salt, and fresh pepper.

"Does your grandmother make lasagna and stuff?" Celia asked.

"Sometimes," Danielle said. "But that's kind of American Italian. Nonna makes more real Italian stuff, southern Italian like her mother taught her. I know she'd love to cook for you guys. We could have dinner at my house next week."

Later, slugging down her third piece of Nonna's tiramisu (creamy, chocolaty, way better than anything she'd ever had in a restaurant), Junie agreed that dinner with Danielle's grandmother was a fine idea. The kitchen was hot and the back of her neck felt damp, like after a nice jog on a sunny day. And she felt something close to the adrenaline rush that she got from running, that feeling of confidence and accomplishment.

After the girls had wiped the spilled tomato sauce from the counter, the burned bits from the range, the stray noodles from the table, after they had spritzed every available surface with Lysol and piled the dishes in the dishwasher, after they had traded Aretha Franklin for Danielle's Missy Elliott and then again for Junie's Cat Power, Danielle and Celia said good-bye at the doorway. "So we'll do this again next week?" Celia said.

"Definitely," Danielle said. "I'll talk to Nonna about it tonight. Maybe next Friday."

Once her friends had disappeared into the drizzly night, Junie made herself a cup of tea. She was still wearing the apron, but now it was stained and discolored with grease, with red and brown splotches all over the front and two basil leaves smushed on one of the straps. She sat down in an armchair by the back windows and looked out into the tiny yard, where a stray cat was scratching in the grass. The kitchen air still smelled like garlic and basil, and the CD player had rotated to Junie's father's Frank Sinatra.

When Frank was finished singing, and the cat had disappeared, and her cup of tea was empty, Junie stood up and stretched out her arms. It was a good way to end a happy night. She tossed the filthy apron in the washing machine and headed upstairs to bed.

Orange Juice,
Cappuccino,
and
Gwen Stefani

At six-thirty on Saturday morning, before Yogilates, Celia slipped into her kimono and tiptoed into the kitchen, careful not to make any noise that could rouse Max. She poured herself a glass of orange juice and sat down at the kitchen table, breathing meditative breaths in order to start her day with positivity.

"Oh, my, but don't you get up early!" exclaimed a cheery British voice behind her.

Celia nearly spit out her juice.

"Sorry, darling, didn't mean to scare you. Have to get back early to walk my Ginger. Your father sleeps so soundly! I hardly think he knows I've left. What a lovely kimono you're wearing!"

Celia forced herself to swallow. "What—?" She took a deep breath and attempted to regain her center. "Jane, it's such a surprise to see you. What are you doing here?"

"Well, what do you think I'm doing here?" Jane asked brightly, and Celia winced with disgust. "Max and I went out for dinner, had a lovely evening, one thing led to another, and what do you know? It's Saturday morning and I'm in Brooklyn! Hilarious, really. Totally unexpected."

Jane opened the refrigerator and took out the jug of homemade fresh-squeezed orange juice, pouring herself a glass as comfortably as if she'd lived in this apartment her whole life. She was wearing a black cocktail dress and heels, and she had thick rings of last night's makeup smudged below her eyes like an exhausted hooker.

"I didn't realize that you and my father went out last night," Celia said, willing her voice to sound calm.

"Well, we were staying late at the gallery, planning for the show, and then we felt hungry—and you know how one thing can lead to another, darling, don't you? I mean, you're a big girl, right?" Jane glugged down her juice.

"You know what, Jane, I have to get dressed for Yogilates now. It's been so nice to—"

"Darling, wait. I have a favor to ask you before you run off." Jane leaned forward. "My nephew, Henry, is about your age, and he's going to be in New York from London for a month or so, and frankly I'm so busy with the gallery and with . . . Well, anyway, I was wondering if you would be so good as to perhaps spend a little time with him while he's here. He's tremendously good fun, I promise you."

"You want me to babysit your nephew?" Celia asked. Showing up in her kitchen at six-thirty on a Saturday morning to ask for a favor! This woman had some nerve on her.

"It would hardly be babysitting, dear. Henry is nineteen and quite self-sufficient. His father is Pakistani and I think they just raise them that way."

Celia couldn't bear to be in the room with Jane for a second longer. "Fine. I mean, sure."

"Oh, brilliant!" Jane said. "That really is quite lovely of you, dear. I'll give him your number. He'll be so thrilled!"

The sun shone down on her head, but Celia walked to Yogilates in a state of utter gloom. Thinking about it now, she found it unbelievable that in the fourteen years she had lived alone with her father, she had never encountered another woman in the house early in the morning. Yet she hadn't, and the shock of it—above and beyond the shock of that woman being *Jane*—felt like enough to send her to bed for the rest of the day.

Celia could barely remember her mother, and whatever dim memories she had—a flash of her lighting candles at some long-ago party, watching her buy popcorn at the circus—were too distant to mean much. There were photo albums, of course, and in the seventh grade Celia had gone through a phase of studying those albums every night. But the photographs never told Celia what her mother's laugh sounded like, or whether or not she told a good bedtime story, or what it felt like to give her a hug. Her name was Kathy, and she'd died in a car accident five days after Celia's third birthday, visiting her sister down in Georgia. They flew the body back up to Brooklyn, and Celia stayed with a babysitter while everyone else went to the funeral.

Sometimes, when she was younger, Celia liked to ask her father questions about her mother. What was her favorite music, what was her favorite color, did she like to dance or sing or play sports? "Jazz, purple, she couldn't really sing, but she sure liked to dance." He never said much more than that, and after all these years, not talking about her had become a habit between them.

Celia wondered what her mother would think if she could meet Jane. She'd probably think she was pretentious and fake, a Twinkie who thought it was terribly *branché* to date a black sculptor. She'd see right through Jane's accent and her high heels and her art gallery. Or maybe she'd be more forgiving about Jane and just be glad that Max seemed happy?

Oh, this was a stupid line of reasoning. Celia's mother was dead. She had no opinions.

It was a few minutes before eight when she arrived at the Carroll Gardens Community Center. The sun was still shining, and a warm wind blew through the tops of the trees. When Celia was younger, she liked to imagine that her mother was all around her, in the air, in the sky, in the leaves. Celia wished she could still imagine that because this morning, she felt so alone.

Junie and Celia met at Third Street Sports after class. Despite two hours of chanting, deep breathing, and saluting the sun, Celia was still freaking out.

"I have to admit, that's pretty disgusting," Junie said. "How weird to think of Max, like, doing it."

"Please. On the one hand, I guess I'm happy for him, but on the other hand, couldn't he have just waited till I left for college?"

"I know. It's only another year and a half."

It was later that Saturday and the two girls were shopping for sneakers; well, Junie was shopping for sneakers, tending to her broken heart with a little retail therapy, and Celia was eyeing a sparkly purple yoga mat. "Do you think your parents still do it?" Celia asked.

"If they do, it's phone sex," Junie said. "They're never in the same country long enough to have it any other way."

"Sad."

"I guess, but maybe it keeps their marriage strong. I mean, absence makes the heart grow fonder and blah blah blah." Junie slid her feet into a pair of gray Saucony sneakers. For school-day wear, she preferred New Balance, and she had a pair of old red Converse low-tops that she wore once in a while to spice up her look. But for track practice or even just casual jogs around the neighborhood, Junie preferred Saucony. She jumped up and jogged in place for a minute. "These feel good," she said.

Celia was still staring at the yoga mat, but her head was clearly somewhere else. "You've got to see her, Junie. I mean, she's like a parody of a British woman, you know? It's all *dahling* this and *lovely* that, and her hair's dyed and teased, and she wears these slutty little black suits."

"What's so British about a slutty black suit?"

"Girl! Don't disagree with me!" Celia said. "And then she has the absolute nerve—the *audacity*—to ask me if I'll hang out with some nephew of hers who's coming to town. Like it's not enough that she just *shows* up in my kitchen at ass o'clock in the morning, but then she wants me to babysit?"

"Babysitting? Really?" Junie asked, still jumping up and down in her sneakers, testing the fit.

"Babysitting!" Celia exploded. "And now I feel so awkward, like what am I going to say to my father when I see him? Do I pretend that I don't know? Do I act like it's totally normal to see Jane in our house at the crack of dawn?"

"You should just ask him what's up," Junie said, heading to the cash register with the sneakers under her arm. "If Jane is really going to be in his life, then he's probably going to want to talk to you about it."

Celia shivered with disgust, and Junie couldn't help but wonder if her reaction to her father's fling was as much about jealousy or possessiveness of Max as it was about dislike of Jane. After all, it had been Cee and Max alone in that house ever since she was three years old. She'd never had to compete for Max's heart before.

"What are you thinking about?" Celia asked.

"Oh, nothing, *dahling*. It's just amazing how expensive everything's gotten these days, even out here in *fabulous* Brooklyn." Junie looked down at her credit card slip—she hadn't realized she was spending one hundred dollars of her parents' hard-earned money.

"That's another thing!" Celia exclaimed. "I've been begging my dad to let me take him shopping for his gallery opening. If he goes with Jane instead of me, I'll completely bug."

"You're already bugging," Junie pointed out.

"True," Celia said. "Let's get some coffee."

"That'd be *lovely*," Junie said, and Celia elbowed her in the side.

Steve Reese was behind the counter at the Coffee Carriage, wearing a bright orange T-shirt that said I LOVE TACOS and sporting the faint outlines of a goatee. He was talking animatedly to a woman on the customer side of the counter, a tall, skinny redhead with a nose ring and a leather vest. Celia and Junie had planted themselves near the counter, at the round table with the chipped mosaic top. The resident tabby crawled up on Celia's lap, but Celia, allergic, picked the cat up like she was a piece of veal and passed her over to Junie.

A waitress came up and took their order since Steve was still lost in conversation with the redhead.

"I wonder what Danielle's up to today?" Celia asked loudly after the waitress disappeared, but Steve didn't even turn his head. "Man," Celia whispered. "You know he can hear me."

"Yes, it would be nice if our friend Danielle were here with us today, wouldn't it?" Junie said even more loudly, but again Steve didn't even glance in their direction.

"I wonder if he even remembers her," Junie said as the waitress delivered their drinks. "He looks like such a player."

"He's shady. You can tell just by looking at him."

"Well, maybe not exactly shady . . ." Junie said, cocking an eyebrow. Celia thought that most men were shady just by looking at them. It was odd when you considered that Celia had been raised by a gentle, loving man, who, if anything, should have taught her that men were not universally creeps. But Celia was fairly suspicious of all of them, save her father. It was her well-kept secret that she'd never even kissed one; Junie was the only person in the world who knew that.

"Speaking of evil men," Celia said, "have you spoken to Brian?"

"Not in four days," Junie said. "Can you believe it? Eleven months of total togetherness and now nothing."

"What's it like at school?"

"We ignore each other," Junie said. "Or we sort of nod and pretend we're the faintest of acquaintances."

"Sounds very mature."

"I still miss him, though. I know I'm doing a good job of acting like everything's cool, but it's been hard for me to sleep at night and—" Junie sighed and blew on her drink. "I keep wondering if I should just call him and make it better."

"Actually, I think it's high time *he* called *you!*"

"Hey, guys! What are you doing here?" It was Danielle, bright eyed and smiling. She smelled strongly of floral perfume.

"Hey!" Junie said. She didn't mind being interrupted just before one of Celia's lectures. "We were just talking about you! Sit down!"

Danielle looked up and over at Steve, who was still speaking intently to the redhead. She sat down with them and dropped her purse on the floor. "I know her," she said. "She used to sing with their band. She had this whiny little-girl voice and eventually they kicked her out to go in a tougher direction. They didn't need like a Gwen Stefani, you know? Her B-flats sounded like C-sharps."

"I see," Junie said. She didn't mention that Steve had been talking to that Gwen Stefani for over twenty minutes, dedicating so much attention to their conversation that his customers were giving up hope of ever receiving their coffees.

"You look good, by the way," Celia said. It was true— Danielle was wearing low-riding jeans and a white tank, and her hair was loose down her back.

"Oh, well, not that it matters or anything if Steve isn't even *looking in my direction*."

"What happened with him the other night, anyway?"

"Hmmm . . . ?" Danielle said blandly. "Oh, you know, we just hung out late. It was cool." But her casual tone was betrayed by the anxious glances she shot in Steve's direction. Junie felt sorry for her. Sometimes she seemed rather old, but right now Danielle seemed so young.

Just then the redhead turned and marched out of the Coffee Carriage, and Steve looked up and noticed Danielle. He smiled a big cheery smile and came over for a chat.

"Hey, you!" he said, this time giving Celia and Junie the courtesy of a nod. He crouched down by Danielle's chair. "I was just talking to Skye about her coming back to the group. Remember her? Shrub wants to add female vocals again and she doesn't have any projects going on now, so we were thinking—" He reached up and touched her on the chin. "You smell good."

"Could I get a cappuccino?" Danielle said airily. "I would've come over to order, but you were so *enthralled* in your conversation with Skye, and I didn't want to interrupt."

"C'mon," Steve said gently. "Don't be like that."

"Could I just get a cappuccino, please?"

"Yeah," he said, and turned to Celia and Junie. "You two want anything? This round's on me. An apology for being so . . . enthralled before."

"Ooh, in that case, another mocha latte," Junie said.

"Make that two."

As Steve headed off with their order, Celia shook her head in amusement. "Men," she said. "Between Brian, Steve, and my father, I think the whole species is an enormous waste of oxygen."

"What happened with your father?" Danielle asked.

"I caught a woman leaving our house this morning. She spent the night with my dad. And she's like a complete idiot."

"Really," Danielle said, her eyes open wide. "Well, I guess it's good that your dad's getting some, even if it's with a moron. The last person my mother slept with was my father, and that was in like 1980-something. Although according to her, he was an idiot too."

"So my father and your mother have something in common."

Steve reappeared with their drinks carefully balanced on a tray. Speaking of idiots, Junie thought.

Celia spent Sunday and Monday doing her best to avoid Max. She taught extra tumbling classes, took Monday night yoga, and did her studying at Junie's house instead of in the kitchen. But on Tuesday evening Max caught her as she was heading out the door.

"Hey, stranger," he said, wiping his hands on his baggy white smock.

"Hey," Celia said.

They were in the kitchen; Max poured himself a glass of water and offered her one. "So you want to tell me why you've been sneaking around the past couple of days? You haven't even been home for dinner."

When confronted with a direct challenge, Celia liked to respond honestly, but in this case she didn't know exactly what to say. She paused for a second and looked at the bags under her father's eyes. "Well, you haven't actually been around that much either, right? I mean, this gallery show's been taking up a lot of your time."

"That's true," Max said. He took a sip of his water and stared into his glass for a moment. "Are you sure this doesn't have anything to do with Jane?"

"Jane?" Celia said. "Why would it?"

"She mentioned to me that she saw you the other morning. I was waiting for you to say something about it."

"Well, I was waiting for *you* to say something about it."

"What would you like me to say exactly, Celia? That you don't like her, so I won't spend time with her? Or to promise that I'll only make future romantic decisions based on your approval?"

Celia was flabbergasted. "That's not what I said, Dad! What's wrong with you?"

"Don't take that tone with me," Max said, but there was more sadness in his voice than anger.

"What tone are you talking about?"

"Celia," Max said, and that was all. The kitchen was filled with dark silence.

"Look," Celia said, trying to bring some composure back to the conversation. "It's just that I'd never seen a woman here early in the morning. I was surprised is all."

Max nodded but stayed quiet. He drained his glass of water and then refilled it. Finally he said, "I like her, Celia."

"Really?"

"Really," Max said heavily. He put his hands on Celia's shoulders; he was one of the few people she knew who was tall enough to have to bend down to look her in the eye. "But she'll never replace you in my heart, Cee. You're my girl."

"Give me a break, Dad. That's not what I'm worried about."

"Well, what is it, then?"

Celia shrugged out of her father's hands and picked up her Walkman. "I don't know. I don't feel like talking about it. I'm going out."

As she closed the door behind her, she could see Max looking down at his oversized hands.

Fiori
e
Ragazze

"So who's coming again?" Nonna asked. She had dressed up for Friday night dinner, exchanging her housecoat for a gray cotton dress and taking the rollers out of her hair. She'd even dabbed on a little pink lipstick.

"My friend Celia, Grandma. From school. She lives up the street, remember I told you?"

"I remember. I'm not senile." Nonna fluffed some flowers in the vase on the dining room table. "And who else?"

"Junie Goldstein. She's Celia's friend from growing up. She goes to Brooklyn Prep."

"Are they gonna like our kind of food?" Nonna asked, moving heavily toward the kitchen. She had planned a grand feast for the girls: eggplant rollatini, broccoli rabe with raisins, caramelized oranges, and a braised shank of lamb. Rita and Christina were joining the dinner tonight, as was Mrs. Lucci, their next-door neighbor and Nonna's best friend.

"They totally love Italian food. You should have seen what we did to your tiramisu last week."

Nonna gave Danielle a wry smile. "What exactly did you do to it, *bella*?"

"Ate it. But, like, with a lot of enthusiasm."

"*Bene.* I like healthy eaters."

Danielle had set the table in the formal dining room with the heavy porcelain plates, the old silver-plate cutlery, the thick crystal wine goblets. She had parted the purple velvet curtains to let sunshine into the room. She'd dusted the sideboard and Nonna's ugly old china and the pictures that hung on the wall (portraits of her dead grandfather and her dead uncle, both in their army uniforms).

Celia and Junie arrived at six o'clock, Junie with a bouquet of daisies for Nonna, Celia with a jug of ginger beer.

"Welcome!" Danielle didn't want to admit that she was nervous about showing Celia and Junie her house. They both lived in such swanky places, with fancy modern furniture and lots of light. Danielle's house was the exact opposite: old, dark, and jammed with half-rotting wood bureaus and tables.

But she needn't have worried. "You have so much cool stuff!" Junie said as Danielle showed them around. Together she and Celia oohed and aahed over the old-fashioned furnishings: the lace doilies, the elaborate moldings, the fading Oriental rugs. "It's like something from Poe!" Junie whispered as Danielle led them into the kitchen.

"Is that good?" Danielle asked.

"Oh yeah," Junie said. "Very dramatic."

"Così siete arrivate!" Nonna said as the girls entered the kitchen. "You're here!"

"It's nice to meet you," Celia said, holding out her hand for Nonna to shake. But she ignored it and instead got up on a little step stool to give Celia a fat kiss on the cheek. *"Mio dio, come sei alta,"* she said, before handing her an apron. "So tall!" Celia laughed. She was a good foot taller than Danielle's grandmother.

Climbing back down off the step stool, she turned to face Junie. "And what are these?" she said, her brown eyes sparkling. "Daisies?" Nonna held the flowers to her nose and sniffed twice.

"I hope you like them. I don't think they smell like anything," Junie offered.

"Are you crazy? *Fiori?* They smell delicious!" And with that, she pinched Junie's face in her hands and kissed her on the cheek. Up close, Nonna gave off a faint scent of cold medicine, and her hands were twisted and gnarled from arthritis.

"So are you done freaking out my friends, Nonna?" Danielle asked. "Can we get started?"

"Freaking out your friends? I don't understand how you're talking," Nonna said as Junie wiped Nonna's lipstick off her cheek.

The girls prepared the lamb shank first. Nonna preheated the oven and seasoned the lamb, an awkward, fleshy hunk of it, with lots of salt and pepper. "Celia, *cara,* put some of this tomato paste in a pot. What are you afraid of? It won't bite.

Now hurry, *prego,* add those herbs by the stove top, and Junie, that garlic you chopped? Give it to your tall friend over here. Cook it for three minutes. And don't be scared, *cara,* you're doing beautifully." Danielle couldn't help but laugh at the nervous look on Celia's usually composed face.

"Danielle, stop giggling. I want you to mix up the red wine and the broth in a bowl. Add a pinch of sugar. Do you know what a pinch looks like?"

"What should I do?" Junie asked.

"You watch. Come here." And so Junie watched as Celia simmered the herbs and the garlic, Danielle mixed the wine, broth, and sugar, and then Nonna poured the liquid into Celia's pot. "Junie, your turn. I want you to pick up that nice piece of lamb, *bambina,* and plop it down in here. Use that big fork over there. And add some oil." Junie froze, unable to imagine negotiating the unwieldy chunk of lamb with a fork. "What are you waiting for? Our herbs are gonna burn. Let's go," Nonna said, patting Junie's arm. Her gnarled hands were surprisingly soft.

Just then the doorbell rang, and Danielle ran off to answer it, reappearing with a twenty-something-looking guy with black curly hair and coffee-colored eyes. He had tan skin and a bumpy nose and was dressed entirely in white.

"Roberto!" Nonna cried excitedly, dropping her spoon to give the boy a hug and a kiss on each side of his face. "What have you brought for me?"

"Guys, this is my cousin Rob," Danielle said. "Rob, this is Celia and Junie."

"Nice to meet you," Rob said. "It smells delicious in here. What is that, osso buco?"

"Lamb shank," Junie offered. This guy was really cute.

"That's what osso buco is, sweetheart," Nonna said sharply, and Junie blushed.

"Well, it really does smell great, osso buco, lamb shank, whatever," Rob said, winking at Junie, who blushed even harder. "Here's the ricotta you asked for, Zia Maria. I'm sorry I can't stay for dinner, but I've got to run a couple more errands before eight."

"Errands, what errands? Stay for a glass of wine at least, *bambino*."

"The Ragazzis need two pounds of mozzarella, I've got to drop off a wheel of parmesan at Fra Antelli, and that pastry shop on Henry needs fresh whipping cream. And I'm running late already. But thanks for the offer."

"So before you leave us, tell me how your father is doing."

"He's fine, Zia."

"So fine he can't pick up the phone and call me once in a while?"

"I'll tell him to call you," Rob said, and backed up through the kitchen door. "But I've really got to go now. It was nice to meet you guys. Enjoy your dinner," he said, smiling right at Junie, who stared after him wistfully as he disappeared.

"Oh my God, you're totally sweating him," Danielle said as soon as he was gone.

"Am not!" Junie said. She returned to her cutting board and crushed a piece of garlic.

"You *so* are. You're blushing so hard! Isn't she blushing, Celia?"

"You're blushing."

"Well, of course she is," Nonna interjected. "Roberto is adorable. You'd have to be blind not to notice him. And such a good boy," Nonna said, scowling in Danielle's direction. "Not a liar and a cheater, like most boys his age."

"Not all boys are liars and cheaters, Nonna," Danielle muttered, adding olive oil to a cast-iron pot.

Nonna shook her head. "Not all," she said. "But a lot. I know young men. Believe me, I know more than you could imagine." Nonna straightened her heavy gray dress and waved a hand in front of her face. The kitchen was already starting to get warm, and Nonna's face looked a little gray.

Junie flashed back to Mrs. Finnegan: *Young people don't know what old age is, and old people forget what youth was.*

She wondered if Danielle's cousin Rob ever took a break from being a good boy to have a little fun. Then, realizing she was blushing again, she turned back toward the simmering pot.

An hour later they set the food on the table. Rita and Christina had returned from Macy's looking exhausted, but Rita still managed to put the finishing touches on the eggplant (a drizzle of oil, a sprinkle of salt) and Christina helped the girls bring the food out to the dining room. Their neighbor, Mrs. Lucci, even shorter than Nonna, arrived with a cut-glass bowl of zabaglione. "The strawberries are no good yet," she said instead of "hello." "So we ain't gonna eat it with strawberries."

"Hello, Mrs. Lucci!" Danielle, Rita, and Christina called.

"Hello, girls, hello. So nice of you to have me here for dinner. I don't get many social invitations these days, certainly not for a nice dinner party with all these young people." Mrs. Lucci smiled at Junie. "You're going to have to move over, young lady. You're sitting in my seat."

Steam was rising from the dishes on the table as the seven women dove into the food. "Oh my God," Junie said as the eggplant melted on her tongue. "This is so totally delicious." The girls washed their dinner down with Max's ginger beer while Rita, Christina, Nonna, and Mrs. Lucci poured generously from a decanter of red wine that sat on the sideboard.

By the time the dinner plates were cleared and the zabaglione sat on the sauce-splashed table, the girls were moaning with food fatigue. Junie had taken off her sweater and was just wearing her thin tank top, and Celia was leaning back in her chair as if she was about to pass out.

"So Danielle," Mrs. Lucci said, picking at her teeth with the tine of a fork. "Who's the new boyfriend?"

"Excuse me?"

Mrs. Lucci grinned devilishly. "I was at the laundromat the other afternoon and I see you walking down the street arm in arm with some tattooed guy. I try calling to you— Danielle! Danielle!—but this one's so lost in love she don't even look up."

"A guy with tattoos?" Christina asked. "Who's that, D.?"

"It's nobody," Danielle said, burning. She couldn't believe Mrs. Lucci was just blowing her secrets into the air this way. Celia and Junie both reached for their water glasses at the same time, avoiding Danielle's eyes.

"Oh, he was a looker, that one. Like a James Dean, maybe. The dangerous type." Mrs. Lucci cackled.

"Danielle, you're not seeing that jerk Steve Reese again, are you?" Christina asked, her big cow eyes opening wide. "I can't believe you'd start hanging out with that jerk after everything he—"

"He's not a jerk."

"Your memory is dangerously short, Danielle," Christina said.

"The one with the tattoos!" Nonna shrieked, finally catching on. "The one who made you cry?"

"I can't believe you'd go out with him again!" Christina said. "Not after everything—"

"Oh, screw me for having a life, Christina."

"Such foul language!" sniffed Mrs. Lucci.

"Are you forgetting what you walked in on, Danielle? Are you forgetting what you *saw*?" Christina's face was red. Junie and Celia shifted in their chairs.

"What did she see?" Mrs. Lucci asked nobody in particular.

"Now, everyone," Rita said. "I don't think it's fair for any of us to pick on poor Danielle for making bad choices about men. God knows we've all made our own bad choices too. . . ."

Junie spoke up suddenly. "Actually, I think it's possible Steve's changed," she said. All eyes turned to her, and Junie swallowed hard. "I mean, I met him a couple of times this week and I think he seems pretty cool."

"Yeah," Celia backed her up. "He got us free lattes at the Coffee Carriage this week."

There was silence for a moment as each woman considered their testimony.

Danielle's eyes were moist with gratitude. "See? I told you guys, he's changed."

"I'm sure he has," Christina sneered.

"Well, I don't like anybody who makes my Daniella cry," Nonna said. With that, she picked up her plate and headed toward the kitchen.

Snickers Bars,
Sushi,
and
Scrambled Eggs

On Tuesday afternoons Celia taught beginner tumbling to local kids at the community center. There were only five girls in the class; however, their average age was six years old and they required intense personal management. Splits, somersaults, cartwheels—none of it was that difficult, but when Brianna pulled on Jessica's braid and then Sophie started to cry because Zoe called her "fatty fat," Celia felt her positivity start to leak out through her shoes and disappear into the center's shiny wooden floors.

"Brianna, you go to that corner. Jessica, you go to that one over there. Today we're going to practice meditation. Do you guys know what meditation is? It's sitting very quietly and thinking as hard as you can. Got it? Very quietly. *Starting now.*"

But despite the fifteen minutes of fidgety meditation at the end of class, Celia left the community center drained.

She didn't believe in processed food as a rule, but she needed quick energy; she bought a jumbo-size Snickers at the bodega on her corner and tore into it like a hungry carnivore. She chewed greedily, her mouth open, and was in mid-bite when she reached her front door.

There was a boy in the hallway, loitering in front of her apartment. He was wearing a neon orange windbreaker and listening to an iPod, his hair flopping in front of his eyes. He was about two inches shorter than Celia.

She quickly wiped the chocolate from her mouth. "May I help you?"

"I'm Henry," the boy—well, young man—said in a strong British accent. "You're Celia, right? My aunt Jane told me I should meet you here today." He looked down at his watch. "Seems to me you're a bit late, aren't you?"

Oh God, Celia thought. Not this. Not today. "Jane didn't . . . I wasn't . . ." she said, and then stopped to take a breath. "Jane never told me that you were coming today, exactly. How long have you been waiting here? How'd you get in?"

"Someone was leaving as I came to the door," he said. He pulled his headphones off his ears. "According to Jane, you were to expect me around four-thirty."

"Well, that's pretty interesting because Jane never said a word to me." She jammed the rest of the chocolate bar into her pocket. Damn that British twit and her stupid, invasive, conniving ideas. Celia did her best not to mutter to herself as she searched for her keys.

"Would you rather I just left, then? I don't want to be any

trouble," he said. "You seem to be rather unprepared for guests, so . . ."

"Look, I'm sorry, but on Tuesdays, I teach gymnastics to kids. It's totally grueling, and it uses up all my energy, and I wasn't expecting you."

"So I should leave?" Henry said, tugging at his iPod.

Celia sized him up. He seemed harmless enough: skinny, slightly bug-eyed, with light brown skin and shiny black hair. Under the windbreaker he wore a pale pink shirt, which totally clashed, but whatever. Anyway, he'd schlepped all the way here and had waited for forty-five minutes—how could she send him home?

"Look, forget it. You came out all this way," Celia said. "Come on in."

Henry wandered among Max's sculptures while Celia washed the chocolate off her hands and changed out of her sweatpants. She found him in the living room, bobbing his head to whatever was on his iPod, his eyes half closed.

"What are you listening to?" she said. He popped open his eyes and looked at her blankly. "I said, *what are you listening to?*"

"Oh, right. This." Henry pulled the headphones off his ears. "Nobukazu Takemura. Do you know it? It's bloody brilliant. Electronica, mostly."

Celia shook her head. As far as she was concerned, electronics didn't make music; people did. But if this guy liked electronica, then maybe he'd like to hang out in the East Village, one of the most techno-friendly neighborhoods in the city—and only five stops away on the F train. "Listen, I was thinking we could go to the East Village for an hour or two. They've got music stores and stuff. That okay with you?"

"Ah, brilliant," Henry said. "Do you think we could find some DJ equipment? I've been looking for this Japanese mixing board, the Yamaha MG 16/4. . . ."

"I have no idea about that, but we could definitely look." Celia threw a long knit scarf around her neck and grabbed her purse. As far as she was concerned, she was being a Good Samaritan, helping a dorky British tourist find his way around New York. She'd give it two hours, no more. "Come on, Henry. Let's get out of here."

At Shrine Records on East Ninth Street, Henry lost himself in a jungle of used vinyl, stacking up his choices in a pile on the counter and then returning for more. Celia watched as he dug through the rows of Front Line Assembly, Delerium, Ministry, Pacobel. "I can't believe how much industrial they stock here!" he said gleefully.

"I guess you spin?" Celia had little interest in any of the music stocked at Shrine Records, but she wanted to make conversation.

"I do, yeah. Weeknights at a small club in Reading. Mostly industrial, house, drum and bass, some garage." He pronounced *garage* with the emphasis on the first syllable. "But good cheap vinyl is thin on the ground in London. We just don't get a selection like this anywhere, not even Rough Trade."

Celia reached into a bin and pulled out a record at random. "What do you think of this one?" she asked.

"A twelve-inch *Computerwelt*, by Kraftwerk? The German

edition?" Henry's eyes opened wide. "Celia, that's genius! Do you know this band?"

"Not at all."

"They're like the forerunners of most modern industrial. Really brilliant! Do you mind if I take it?"

What a geek, Celia thought. "Henry, be my guest."

"Christ!" he exclaimed a second later. "A Japanese promo of *Papa's Got a Brand New Pigbag*! 1981! I can't believe this was just hidden here!"

"Henry, don't you ever listen to real music? With human vocalists? Actual instruments?"

Henry shrugged and added *Pigbag* to his pile. "I find that stuff rather boring," he said. "It's what people listened to two hundred years ago. Electronica is the musical medium of tomorrow, you know? Why be stuck in the past when you can listen to the future?"

"I don't think listening to real singers playing real instruments means being stuck in the past," Celia said, doing her best not to get irritated.

"Someday you will." Henry shrugged, returning to his records.

On the four-block walk back to the subway Henry read the backs of the sleeves of his new albums, stumbling over the cracks in the sidewalk. Celia wanted nothing more than to be rid of him, but she figured that for the few more minutes they were together, she might as well pump him for info about Jane.

"So, listen, has your aunt ever been married?" Celia asked. "Notable boyfriends, anything like that?"

"Hmmm?" Henry said, slipping *Computerwelt* back into the yellow Shrine Records bag. "No, I don't think so. I mean, she's dated around like anyone else, but she never seemed to get too serious with anyone." Waiting for the light to change on Avenue A, Henry contemplated. "She does seem to fancy your father, though."

"What do you mean?"

"Fancies him, you know. She didn't stop talking about him all morning. Loves his sculpture, thinks he's the nicest man she's ever met, et cetera."

"Well, he *is* the nicest man she's ever met," Celia said defensively. "He's a really good person. He cares about people." And then she felt a wave of sadness wash over her because she hadn't been particularly generous with Max lately, and she knew her father felt hurt.

When she got home, she called for Max; she wanted to give him a hug. But he was gone for the evening, with just a note on the kitchen table: *I'll be late at the studio, gotta finish up this project. There's roast chicken in the fridge. Love, Dad.*

Of course Steve had nothing to eat in his apartment. "Shrub finished off my Rice Krispies."

"Rice Krispies don't count as real food anyway," Danielle said. "Do you have any spaghetti, maybe?" After two hours of rolling around on the bed with Steve, she was famished. Besides, since Danielle could barely stand the cafeteria food at school and students weren't allowed to leave campus for lunch (a fact of St. Margaret's life that was even more infuriating than their stupid uniforms), she hadn't eaten since breakfast. "Or don't you have Pop-Tarts or a loaf of bread or anything?"

"Nah," Steve said, running his hand under her shirt. "Usually I just eat whatever's left over at the Coffee Carriage."

"So you live on pastries?"

Steve grinned up at her and licked his lips. They were lying on his futon, both half dressed. "Yep."

"That's ridiculous." Danielle got up, pulled on her skirt, and marched to the kitchen, which was, considering the state of the rest of the apartment, surprisingly orderly. There were a few dishes in the sink, and the floor was dirty, but the countertops looked scrubbed and someone had recently taken out the garbage. Danielle opened the refrigerator: a six-pack of Bud, a two-liter bottle of Coke, a jar of mustard, a stick of butter, and an unopened can of olives. Resting in the egg compartment on the refrigerator door were seven large white eggs. Good enough, Danielle thought.

She dug up a frying pan from one of the kitchen cabinets, melted some butter, and cracked open four eggs into a clean-ish bowl. Whisking them with a fork, she sprinkled in some salt and pepper from kitchen-table shakers and scrambled them in the melted butter. She opened the can of olives, crushed some in her hands, and then added them to the scrambled eggs.

Steve wandered into the kitchen, lazily rubbing his hands on his chest. "Wow, Danielle! That smells awesome."

She took a forkful of eggs and fed it to him. Steve hummed with delight.

"You like?" she asked.

He responded with a long, sexy, eggy kiss.

Danielle got home to find Nonna sitting on her folding chair on the front porch. She was wearing a bulky sweater over her housedress and a scarf tied over her curlers. "Daniella, *cara*, let's take a walk."

"I don't want to, Nonna. I'm tired."

"You're not so tired that you can't walk a little with your grandmother. Come on. I'm an old lady. I need my exercise."

Danielle recognized the determination in Nonna's voice. "Okay," she said, "but not too long. I have to study."

Nonna stood up slowly and drew her sweater close around her shoulders. For a second it struck Danielle how old her grandmother was; how deep the lines in her face were, how dark the bags under her eyes. Despite her ongoing dominance in the kitchen, Nonna really *was* an old lady. She helped her grandmother down the stairs.

It was now twilight, and most of their Carroll Gardens neighbors were in their houses right now, houses just like hers, with old wooden furniture inside and small stoops to sit on and plaster statues of the Virgin Mary on their tiny front lawns. Danielle could smell the pork roasts, veal breasts, tomato gravies, and sage sausages being cooked up in her neighbors' kitchens. She could hear the dim fights of husbands and wives being carried through the windows and walls.

"So what's on your mind, Nonna?" she asked as they walked slowly down Fourth Place, Danielle holding her grandmother's arm.

"I could see you were unhappy the other night. After we said what we had to say about that Steve *carattere*."

"No, Nonna, I understood."

"Don't lie to me, Daniella. I could see from the look on your face you were upset. Hi, Mrs. Rocatello!"

"Hi, Mrs. Bollino!" A gnarled old lady, even older than Nonna, who was sitting on her front lawn, enjoying the starry evening, waved to them.

"So what's your point?" Danielle asked.

"Well, my point is, your mother and your sister and I . . . we know you're a tiny bit different than we are, *bambina*. We look at you and think what a face you have, what a voice—"

"My voice?" The Battaglia women rarely mentioned her voice.

"Look, Danielle, it's just that you're so talented. More than that, you're so beautiful and brave and sometimes we worry. It's only natural. Bravery can turn into stupidity if you're not careful."

"So you think I'm stupid?" Danielle bent down to rub furiously at her knee.

"Oh, Daniella, I'm not calling you stupid." Nonna twined her gnarled hands together. "Sometimes, however, I do worry about your choices. You stay out late, *mia cara*. You hang around with untrustworthy boys. I know you've been coming home past your curfew."

Danielle looked down at the pavement.

"I want you to be careful, *bambina*. I know a little bit more about the world than you think I do and a little bit more about the way men can be. Believe me, I've been there;

I know things you could never imagine about the way men act. And I love you, sweetheart. *Ti amo.* I don't want you to get hurt."

What Danielle wanted to say: No offense, Nonna, but you were married for fifty years and you've been a widow for fifteen. Your husband was an angel who treated you like gold, and these days the only men you know are the ones you watch on your soap operas. *So stop giving me advice you old bag!*

What Danielle actually said: "Okay, Nonna. Whatever."

"You understand me here? You get what I'm trying to tell you?"

Yes, Danielle thought. You want to lock me away at St. Margaret's until it's time to lock me away at Macy's. "I get you, Nonna," she said. "I understand perfectly."

Cuba Libre

That Wednesday, smack in the middle of April, the weather was glorious. Brooklyn Prep girls' long-distance track had a meet the next day, so the team was given the day off to rest, but Junie decided to run anyway—just a mile or two after school. She'd been in a better mood all week and had even started smiling at Brian again, big happy grins in the hallway that he didn't know how to return. What had changed her attitude? Cooking, laughing, and, of course, the sight of Danielle's cousin. She finished the first mile without even noticing, lost in a daydreamy haze.

It was just that he'd been so beautiful. That thick black hair! Those dark brown eyes! Junie was no poet, but she'd spent the better part of the last several evenings thinking in metaphor: his hair is like a dark river—no, his hair is like a wave of chocolate—no, his hair is like chocolate satin—okay, that was ridiculous. But she had never been so struck by the mere sight of a guy before. And while that didn't mean she'd forgotten about Brian, today the thought of him no longer broke her heart.

Brooklyn Prep had some of the largest playing fields of any high school in Brooklyn, and as she ran, she could see a group of boys throwing Frisbees to each other in the field behind the track. Richard Langer, Dan Cho, Bobby Melli, and—yes—Brian, in army supply cutoffs and the blue long-sleeved T-shirt she'd bought for him a few months ago for no particular reason. Without thinking, Junie jogged off the track to where the boys were playing. She watched them toss the Frisbee around for a few minutes, standing partially hidden under the bleachers. Brian was adorable as always, smoothly throwing and catching, running barefoot around the grass. Cho threw the Frisbee his way and Brian caught it with his left hand while running, even though he was a righty. Just then he looked up and noticed Junie watching them.

"Hey," he called, after a surprised moment.

"Hey," she called back. She was still trying to figure out how much she missed him. She was also still trying to figure out if her reaction to Danielle's cousin really meant anything in the context of having loved Brian for so long.

He waved at her awkwardly and then turned to Melli, who was throwing the Frisbee his way. Brian caught it and tossed it quickly to Cho, never once looking back. Junie shrugged, sighed, and started another lap.

On the phone that night Junie attempted some analysis with Celia. "It was the weirdest feeling," Junie said. "Half of me wanted to run after Brian and beg him to come back, and the other half was like, get over it, there are too many other guys out there for me to keep obsessing over my ex-boyfriend."

"Man, I wish I had your optimism," Celia said. She was lying on her bedroom floor, playing with the threads hanging off her fake-Persian rug.

"What do you mean?"

"You think there are so many guys out there to choose from! I'm seventeen years old and I have yet to meet a single guy worth dating."

"Well"—Junie coughed—"that could be because your standards are impossibly high."

Celia snorted. "I don't know what you're talking about."

"Celia, you're holding out for the perfect combination of Lenny Kravitz and Kofi Annan. It's like nothing else will do."

"Don't exaggerate, Junie," Celia huffed. "Look, is it too much to demand a tall, good-looking man? Is it too much to want a brilliant man, a man with good taste in music, a man who respects women in general and me in particular?" She tore the threads off her rug and sighed. "I don't know why I have to settle for another floppy-haired high school boy just 'cause everyone else does."

Junie was silent.

"I mean, no offense."

"Look, Cee, I just think that if you kept your eyes open, you might be surprised at what's out there. If you'll only consider tall, brilliant, non-floppy-haired guys who like the same music you do, you're kind of limiting your options."

"I don't tell you what kind of guys to like, so you shouldn't go around trying to tell me who *I* should like. Besides, I'm sure I'll meet my tall, brilliant Lenny Kravitz–Kofi Annan combo eventually. I have faith."

"Faith is good," Junie conceded. "Just don't let it blind you."

The next morning in chem lab Amanda Begosian was sweatier than usual. "So have you spoken to Brian yet or what?" she asked, as though she and Junie were the type of friends who usually talked about their personal lives. In her safety goggles Amanda looked like a frog. They were doing an experiment called "refluxing," trying to discover a melting point of a certain chemical.

"Not really." Junie could feel a coughing fit coming on and took a swig of Poland Spring to suppress it.

"You okay there, Junie?"

"I'm fine."

Amanda lifted her goggles to scratch the top of her nose. She had big blue eyes, which, when she blinked, projected an air of Bambi-like innocence. "So then I guess you're not going to Richard Langer's party Friday," she said. Richard and Brian were best friends, but Junie had always thought that Richard was her friend too. She'd had no idea there was a party. It stung to be left out.

"I can't," she said smoothly, holding up a test tube to check the level of acid. "I'm hanging out with some friends from a different school," she added, attempting to sound intriguingly vague. "I'm not so into house parties anyway. It's hard for me to run if I've been drinking the night before."

Amanda squinted, adjusted her goggles. "I used to think that too. But remember last month how I came in first in the Empire State regionals? I had been at Maggie McGee's party the night before, and I got so drunk I puked in her parents' bathtub. The next morning? Three K in 14:30."

"That's impossible. You would have been dehydrated."

"I totally wasn't."

"Yeah, but that's not how drinking works," Junie said, willing herself not to fight with Amanda over whether or not a person could get tanked the night before a regional meet and still run three K in under fifteen minutes. It was a physical impossibility, and Junie knew it, but if Amanda wanted to make herself sound like Wonder Woman with a hollow leg, that was her prerogative.

"Sometimes it's just mind over matter, you know what I mean?" The acid was fizzing away in the test tube, and Amanda made some scratch marks in her notebook. "Anyway, it's too bad you won't be at Richard's party. Dan Cho said that Brian was hoping for a reconciliation, although I haven't heard much more about it than that."

Junie closed her eyes for a second and then reopened them. I will not discuss this with Amanda. I will not discuss this. *Remember, lass, lie down with dogs and you'll rise with fleas.* "If Brian wants to reconcile, he knows where to find me."

"True enough," Amanda said airily, and raised the heat on the Bunsen burner. "That is, if he wants to." The compound fizzed up violently, and for a moment Junie hoped it would explode in Amanda's face.

*　　*　　*

The next day during lunch Celia text-messaged Junie and asked if she felt like hosting dinner at her house that night. *In a stupid effort to make peace with my father, I told him I'd hang out with Jane's loser nephew one more time,* she wrote. *I'm such a SUCKER!*

Junie wrote back immediately: *LOL. It's Friday—and you're not meditating tonight? Dahling, that's fabulous. See you at seven. Can't wait to meet Henry.*

At lunch, mulling over menu options, Junie decided on southeast Asian, for no real reason except that Celia had mentioned Henry was part Pakistani. Stopping at a bookstore on the way home after track, Junie dug up an Indian cookbook (was Indian food the same as Pakistani? Was it close enough?) and found directives to purchase garam masala and whole coriander seeds, since these things were the basis of so much Indian cooking. Junie stopped at Key Food and searched for these items, but the store carried neither. Instead she bought coconut milk, curry sauce, and basmati rice, since these ingredients were in the Indian section of the "ethnic" aisle. She also bought vegetables and yogurt.

"I wonder if this guy's even cute," Danielle said. She had arrived twenty minutes early and was poring through the Indian cookbook alongside Junie. "What's his name again? Harry?"

"Henry," Junie said. "And Celia didn't mention whether or not he's cute. It's so weird to even imagine her thinking about guys that way." She wanted to add: And speaking of cute guys, tell me more about your cousin . . . , but she didn't, couldn't bring herself to mention Roberto's name.

"What's Celia's deal, anyway? At school she's kind of aloof, you know? Doesn't really chill with most of us, seems a little snobby. And she dresses so weird. My girls see me hanging out with her lately and they're like, what's up?"

"Oh, I don't know . . ." Junie said, flipping the pages in search of a recipe for chicken tikka. "Cee's always been a little intense. She just believes strongly in the things that are important to her, and that's what she focuses on. But usually, you know, she gets what she wants."

Danielle nodded, then smiled slyly. "Speaking of getting what you want—how hard were you sweating my cousin last week?"

"Excuse me?"

"Don't play dumb," Danielle said. "I saw the way you were checking him out. You should totally come with me to his store tomorrow. We can pick up some groceries for my grandmother."

"Don't you think that'll look obvious?"

"What's to be obvious about if you're not into him?"

Celia arrived a few minutes late accompanied by a bug-eyed boy with a smug smile. He was wearing an obnoxiously bright windbreaker. "I hear we're having a curry," he said, walking into the kitchen like he'd been to Junie's house a million times before.

"Guys, this is Henry, Jane's nephew," Celia said, already sounding mildly irritated. "Henry, meet Junie and Danielle."

"Do you know how to do this curry thing?" Junie asked, waving them both over to the counter. "I bought this cookbook, but it's telling me I'm supposed to make my own cheese?"

"Let's have a look," Henry said, joining Junie and Danielle in front of the cookbook. Celia rolled her eyes and opened the fridge for a glass of water. Junie wished she'd give boys—this boy, any boy—a chance. Henry seemed a bit presumptuous, but that wasn't the worst crime in the world.

"All right, ladies," he said, "this is what we're going to do. You're in luck, you know, since curry happens to be the one thing in the world that I know how to make. You have vegetables?"

"Check," Danielle said, scanning the groceries laid out on the table: fresh broccoli, potatoes, cauliflower, and carrots.

"And I see on the counter that there's curry sauce. Do you have plain yogurt? And rice?"

"Check and check," Danielle said.

"Well done. We're going to make the easiest curry possible this side of London."

"Perfect," said Junie.

Like a British Nonna, Henry soon had the girls hard at work, chopping vegetables, measuring out rice, heating up a sauté pan, and slicing up slivers of lime. Celia put bowls and silverware out on the counter, staying as far away from Henry as she could. In twenty-five minutes the curry was done: it was simply a matter of sautéing the vegetables and then spooning in the curry sauce and the yogurt and serving it all alongside the rice.

"Bachelor food," Henry pronounced, scattering slivers of

lime on each plate. They all took stools along the counter and sat in a row, as if they were eating at a diner: Celia, Junie, Danielle, then Henry.

"This is so spicy!" Danielle shrieked, reaching for a cup of water. "What kind of pepper did you put in it?"

"It's not spicy at all!" Henry laughed. "That's mild curry sauce."

"Dude, get out of here. Pass me more water, Henry."

While Henry refilled the water glasses, Junie turned to Celia. "He seems okay," she mouthed theatrically.

Celia just scowled and pretended not to understand what Junie was saying.

Henry had bought a *Time Out New York* and discovered that one of his favorite bands, a speed-metal hip-hop outfit called Ninja Star, was playing at North Six in Williamsburg that evening. "Come on, ladies, we've got to go. You'll love it."

"I seriously doubt that," Celia said.

"Ah, come on, love," Henry said. "You really should broaden your horizons a bit."

"My horizons are broad enough," Celia said. "And don't call me 'love.'"

"Oh, please, Cee? We never go to clubs!" Junie pleaded. A night out partying would definitely be the cure for her miserable week. And just because Celia wasn't loving Henry was no reason to let her go home early.

"Look, it's a bad idea," Celia said. "I mean, can we even get in? We don't have IDs."

"We'll get in," Danielle said. "We just won't be able to

drink anything." She'd been to clubs all over the city and knew the rules.

"So let's go!" Junie said brightly. "Come on, Cee! It'll be so fun!"

"I'm into it," Danielle said. "I just have to call Nonna and tell her I'll be late. If she ever asks, we were all working on our homework till the middle of the night."

Celia was out of excuses. "Fine," she grumbled. "But I want to be back by midnight. Twelve-thirty at the latest. I've got yoga tomorrow, don't forget."

"How could we forget?" Junie said.

They took a cab to the club, a low building on a dingy block near the waterfront. It was dark and loud and swarming with people, and Henry was nearly busting out of his jacket with excitement. "Oh, this band is spot-on; you guys are going to love it."

"I'd be shocked," Celia muttered.

"I love it already!" Junie said, trying to stay perky.

But the truth was, the place sucked: it was hot and crowded and smelled of smoke and spilled beer. Worse, the music sounded like the noise large animals would make if they were being shaken to death. Celia looked like she was ready to pitch a fit. But Henry and all the other fans at the club (mostly men, Junie noted) were delirious with excitement, jumping up and down and sweating on each other and screaming along with the lyrics. The three girls stood off to the side with their hands over their ears.

"I can't believe you dragged me here!" Celia yelled.

"What?"

"*I said, I CAN'T BELIEVE YOU DRAGGED ME HERE!*" Celia tried again, but Junie just shrugged. It was useless to carry on a conversation in this place. Danielle was checking out every guy who passed her way: the tall ones, the shave-headed ones, the shirtless ones with pierced nipples.

When the show finally ended and the crowd spilled out onto the sidewalk in front of the club, Junie had to hit the side of her head a few times to stop her ears from ringing. The dank air of Williamsburg felt cool and refreshingly clean, and Henry was still bouncing up and down like a maniac. "Supposedly there's an after party with the band down the street! Let's go!"

"You've got to be joking," Celia said.

"Not at all!"

"But I have yoga tomorrow."

"C'mon, it's not even eleven-thirty yet!" Junie enthused, grinning up at Henry, ignoring both Celia's glare and the ringing in her ears. Celia was going to have fun whether she liked it or not. Besides, Junie hadn't thought about Brian in almost two hours now—or almost hadn't, anyway. Williamsburg was a great distraction.

"Let's go, Celia," Henry said, throwing his arm around Celia's shoulders as if they were old friends. Celia winced. "I'll tell you all about the history of speed-metal hip-hop. Come along."

"But I don't *care* about the history of speed-metal hip-hop!" she protested as Henry dragged her up the street toward the party. Danielle and Junie followed, grinning at each other. It was so great to see a guy with his arm around Celia, even if Celia herself seemed to be hating it.

The party was on a rooftop that overlooked the entire Manhattan skyline. It was a clear night, and across the East River the Chrysler Building and the Empire State sparkled with hundreds of white lights. She and Danielle took in the highlights of the New York City view and the lowlight, the spot downtown where the World Trade Towers once stood. Henry and Celia were standing near the musicians, and they seemed to be talking to each other—a good sign.

A card table on the corner of the roof was stocked with bottles of vodka, gin, and rum, and next to the table stood a massive keg. Junie and Danielle went over to the table and looked at it for a second. "What do you think?" Danielle asked.

"Oh, what's the worst one drink could do?" Tomorrow was Saturday, and practice had been canceled at the last minute, so Junie mixed them both rum and Cokes—what she drank at all her cousins' bat mitzvahs—and the two toasted the evening. "Here's to getting out of Cobble Hill."

The crowd looked to be mostly in their twenties or even early thirties—some guys were balding and several of them wore shirts from bowling leagues or auto repair shops. The women were dressed in vintage dresses over jeans or T-shirts with ironic messages on them. They had piercings in their noses, eyebrows, and lips. The men wore glasses with thick rims and battered-looking corduroys. One of them was wearing a skirt.

"Look!" Danielle said, jerking her head toward a woman

with a shaved head decorated entirely in tattoos. "That's so weird! I have to talk to her."

"Talk about what?" But Danielle was off, chasing down the shave-headed girl like a journalist hunting a story. Junie thought that Danielle was the only person she knew who'd be intrigued by a tattooed head rather than grossed out. She had such a weird aesthetic sense: yes to decorated skulls, no to sculptures of dying pigs. Reflecting on this, Junie downed her rum and Coke and poured herself another.

"Cuba Libre?" said a guy to her right, one of the thick-glasses-and-dirty-corduroy types.

"I don't speak Spanish," Junie said.

The guy laughed. "A Cuba Libre is what they call a rum and Coke in Puerto Rico. But you're making yours a little weak, aren't you?"

"I'm not really much of a bartender," Junie said.

"I can tell." The guy splashed a bit more Captain Morgan's into her glass and made a Cuba Libre of his own. "So what's your name?"

"Junie. What's yours?"

"Phil," he said. "I'm the sound guy at North Six."

"Oh," Junie said. "Well, I thought the sound was . . . really great."

Phil laughed. "What do you think of Ninja Star?"

"Ummm . . . it's always good to hear something new."

Phil laughed again. He and Junie ended up talking into the night, about sound ("The secret is to amp the bass"), music ("Okay, well, really I'm more into Cat Power"), and life in New York ("Man, there's nowhere else to live. Except

101

maybe Berlin"). Junie didn't mention that she had just turned seventeen last month, but she assumed that Phil also had things he was keeping to himself. He refilled her Cuba Libres, and she became more expansive, expounding on Indian food, training for a marathon, and her recent breakup with Brian.

"So you're single, then?"

"I guess so." Junie sighed.

"Me too," Phil said. "Girlfriend left me for a drummer a couple of months ago. That's what always happens to the sound guys. Their girlfriends leave them for drummers."

"Is that so?"

"Yep," Phil said, pouring more rum into both their cups. "Only consolation is that drummers' girlfriends usually leave them for the lead singers. So they won't be together too long."

"I guess that's a relief for you," Junie said. Over on one corner of the rooftop she could see Henry talking intently with the two emcees from Ninja Star, his arm still draped casually over Celia's shoulders. In another corner Danielle was lost in animated conversation with Tattooed Skull. Junie sucked down her Cuba Libre (how many had this been? Three? Four?) and put her head in her hands. Just yesterday she had been on such a high horse with Amanda Begosian, and now here she was, getting hammered.

"Why so sad?"

"I'm not sad," Junie said. "I'm drunk." And for some reason this seemed to be exactly what Phil needed to hear, because he put his hand behind her neck and his mouth on hers and stuck his big, fishy tongue in her mouth. Junie was alarmed, but he had his hand on the back of her neck and wouldn't let her come up for air. He leaned into her, breathing hard, his enormous tongue cutting off the air to her windpipe. Junie opened her eyes wide and tried to send psychic signals for Danielle or Cee to come rescue her, but the rooftop refused to carry psychic vibes. She was stuck.

And just then, as Phil was starting to really slobber, Junie felt her stomach heave and the three (or four? Or could it have been five?) Cuba Libres started to dance around her insides. The rooftop began to swim. And before she knew what was happening, Junie felt her throat contract. And then, in the next miserable second, she had puked all over her lap, the floor, her shoes, and poor astonished Phil.

"Sorry?" she said feebly as Celia, Henry, Danielle, and the girl with the tattooed skull came running over to save her.

When Danielle got home, Nonna was sitting up at the kitchen table, watching a rerun of *M.A.S.H.* on the old black-and-white TV. "It's two in the morning, *bambina*. I hope you got your Shakespeare homework done."

"Sure," Danielle said, pouring herself a glass of juice to mask the rum and Coke on her breath.

"You weren't doing your Shakespeare until two in the morning, were you, *bambina*." It wasn't a question.

"I was just hanging out with my girlfriends, Nonna."

"So you lied?"

"I didn't lie," Danielle said coolly. "We did some homework and then we just hung out. It's not like it's a weeknight, Nonna."

"I can't trust you anymore, Daniella."

"Nonna, I was hanging out with my *girlfriends*. It's not like I was with Steve or anything, so don't get hysterical."

"It's past your curfew," Nonna said, and though there was force in her voice, her eyes were red and watery. The old lady was exhausted. Why had she stayed up this late? To try to catch Danielle in a lie? What was the point?

"I called for permission. I told you I'd be late. I have no idea why you're pursuing this." She drained her juice and rinsed out her glass, swelling with indignation.

Nonna shook her head; she looked trapped, somehow, between offense and defense, between wanting to get angry and just wanting to go to bed. "I'm eighty-four years old. I don't know why you have to make me so crazy."

"The only person who makes you crazy is you." Danielle shook her head as she climbed up the stairs. She was so annoyed that she managed to block out the truth: she had lied, and her grandmother knew it.

When Junie got home, she put a bucket next to her bed, grabbed her stuffed Chihuahua, and closed her eyes. The room was spinning. She couldn't believe she had kissed somebody besides Brian—how bizarre was that? How out of the blue! She couldn't remember much about it—was it a good kiss? A bad kiss? It was definitely an older kiss—his cheeks were stubblier than Brian's and his lips felt scratchier somehow. He was definitely the oldest guy she'd ever kissed, by a differential of at least ten years.

Whenever she kissed somebody new, Junie added him to

a mental list that had grown slowly but steadily since she was twelve. The first one was Corey Bergmann at track camp the summer before seventh grade, then Lyle Hendricks on an eighth-grade dare, and then Bobby Melli, her first boyfriend, when she was fourteen; they got all the way to sloppy second before they broke up at the ninth-grade winter dance. Then Rudy Jakes and Mike Yakamura, playing truth or dare at Maggie McGee's house. Then that guy Scott, Maggie's cousin from Australia; they made out every day for two weeks during the winter of her sophomore year before he had to head back to Melbourne. And then, finally, Brian. Brian had been the best kisser of them all, unparalleled, soft but strong and persistent. His breath always smelled good, and his lips always tasted minty, mostly from the Chapstick he applied every ten minutes. She missed kissing Brian. She missed kissing Brian, she missed talking to him, she missed him. That Williamsburg guy was such a loser.

She opened her eyes. The room was no longer spinning.

Carefully leaning over, trying to ignore the ache between her eyes, Junie reached for the phone on her nightstand. She knocked over a carefully stacked arrangement of stuffed animals, winced, and then picked up the receiver. But the buzzing of the dial tone sent a piercing radius of pain through her skull, and she dropped the phone back on its cradle. It was past two in the morning.

She'd talk to Brian on Monday.

Casu
Marzu

At 11 A.M. on Saturday, Celia dragged herself up the stairs to her apartment. Yogilates had been murder; Henry and his stupid concert had kept her out way too late—almost two in the morning! Still, she had to admit that the show had been . . . well, if not fun, definitely interesting. And the after party had turned out to be pretty cool; up on that beautiful roof, even Henry somehow seemed less annoying. Still, even though she hadn't drunk a thing last night (and neither had Henry, she'd noticed), all she wanted to do this morning was light some candles and lie on the floor, practice her breathing, take a nap.

No such luck. Max was waiting for her at the kitchen table, frowning into a cup of coffee.

"Shouldn't you be at the gallery, Dad?"

"Celia, sit down," Max said. He was wearing a polo shirt; that, plus the frown, made him look much more like a traditional dad than he usually did. Where was the smock? The elfin grin? Celia found the whole scene jarring. She sat down.

"Look, Dad, if this is about being late last night, it was only because Jane's nephew wanted—"

"Celia," Max said, cutting her off. His voice was strangely distant, formal. "I don't want to hear you blame Henry or anyone else. You came home at two in the morning. That is totally unacceptable."

"But Dad—"

Max silenced her with a grim look. "Since your mother died, I've had the tremendous responsibility—and pleasure—of raising you. I've always thought there was an agreement between us: I wouldn't be too strict with you, and you wouldn't give me a reason to worry. And until last night we both kept our halves of the agreement."

It occurred to Celia that her father had practiced this speech. "Look, I've never stayed out late before. I didn't drink anything. And it's not like I broke curfew—I don't have a curfew to break!"

"That's my point exactly, Celia. You never had a curfew because I always trusted that you'd be home at a reasonable time. But now that I see you can't be trusted, I'm going to have to be one of those dads I never thought I'd be. From now on, you are to be home by twelve-thirty on weekends and eleven on weeknights. Do you understand me?"

"Dad, what's going on?" Her father had never come down on her like this before, and she had never felt this defensive. It just wasn't their style.

"Why don't you tell me, Celia? Lately you've been sneaking around, you're never home, you've been avoiding me like the worst of the plagues. You're letting me down." His eyes flashed once in anger, and he folded his arms across his massive chest. "And I don't know what to do about it."

"Well, maybe you've let me down a little too, Dad," Celia said, surprising herself. She never spoke to Max in disrespectful tones, but today it seemed the rules were changing.

"Watch yourself, young lady."

"Seriously, Dad. Sneaking around with Jane? Coming home at all hours? Three nights last week you weren't home before I went to bed."

"That's different, Celia. I'm a grown-up. I'm your father."

"How is it different? Isn't it your responsibility to watch out for me?" They were sitting opposite each other at the kitchen table, mirror images of each other, arms folded.

"I don't think I'm abdicating my responsibility toward you by going out on the first few dates I've had in fourteen years."

Celia sighed. "Well, maybe I just think there's a more appropriate way for you to handle your love life."

"And perhaps I think that there's a more appropriate way for you to talk to your father."

"This is bullshit, Dad, and you know it."

"Don't you *ever* use that language with me," Max said. His eyes flashed once more, and his jaw was set with anger.

Oh, this was useless. Celia had never had so much trouble

with her father before. Until Jane came along, she and Max had been a team, honoring each other's privacy while maintaining a friendly understanding.

"You know, this isn't Jane's fault," Max said, as though he'd read her mind.

Celia looked out the window at pigeons resting on the fire escape. "Dad, we didn't fight like this before she came into our lives."

"Well," Max said, "it's possible this fight is long overdue."

Celia wasn't sure what her father meant by that, and she didn't want to ask. She slumped her shoulders, exhausted.

"Take a nap," Max said, releasing her from the kitchen. He stood up heavily and sighed. "I'll wake you in a couple of hours."

Piccolo Dairy was housed in a small storefront on Sullivan Street, on the western edge of SoHo. In the front window hung dried salamis, huge jars of pickled peppers, olives, and cauliflower, boxes of Italian cookies, loaves of Italian bread, and small canisters containing a special holiday cake called panettone. And cheese, of course, enormous wheels of it, stacked up like tires on the front shelves.

Junie hadn't particularly felt like going to meet Rob this afternoon—sure, he'd seemed cute a week ago, cute enough to make her spend a couple of hours daydreaming—but after last night's miserable kiss (and this morning's pounding headache), she didn't think the time was necessarily right for her to start meeting new guys.

"Don't be a baby," Danielle nudged. "Besides, what are

you going to do at home all day? Watch TV and feel sorry for yourself?"

"Come on, Danielle, can't we do it next week?" Even Danielle's voice over the phone made Junie's head ache.

"You're wimping out. . . ."

"Fine, okay, fine." After an hour in a hot bath, two cups of coffee, and three aspirin, Junie felt semi-ready to face the world. She was wearing her standard-issue corduroys and a Brooklyn Prep T-shirt; she didn't have the energy to bust out a cute outfit.

"Hey, ladies!" Rob grinned as they walked into the store. The first thing Junie noticed was that he was still adorable. The dark curls framing his tan face, the muscles bulging under his white T-shirt—she had to actually force herself to look away. She concentrated instead on a long red salami, but then she had to look away from that too. Opera was playing gently in the background.

"Rob, you remember my friend Junie, right?"

"Osso buco," Rob said, sticking his hand out to shake hers. "How could I forget?"

"It's nice to see you again," Junie said, enjoying the feel of his rough palm despite herself. She tried to guess how old he was. Twenty-one? Twenty-two? She wondered if he had a girlfriend that Danielle didn't know about.

"Listen, Nonna needs a pound of buffalo mozzarella, two pounds of tagliatelle, and a quarter pound of pancetta, and she told me that she's paying for it this time and you're not supposed to argue about it."

"Who's arguing?" Rob said, lifting a milky white ball of

mozzarella from a tub. Junie wondered where he got such muscular arms, working with nothing but cheese all day. She hoped they didn't come from, say, lifting his hot girlfriend high in the air during acrobatic sex.

"Here," Rob said to Junie. "Try this."

He sliced her a sliver of mozzarella, still warm from its hot-water bath. The cheese was soft and creamy, slightly tangy, just the faintest bit salty on the outside and tasting on the inside like the essence of pure milk. It was the most delicious cheese Junie had ever tasted. "Oh my God," she said, which felt like an understatement.

"We get milk flown in from a water buffalo farm in Florida," Rob said. "Two deliveries a week, which means two days a week I make real buffalo mozzarella. We're one of the only dairies in the city that does it. Most buffalo mozzarella comes from Italy, but it's always at least two days old by the time it's sold, and the texture just doesn't compare. Of course, mozzarella di bufala doesn't get tough as quickly as regular cow's milk mozzarella, and some people even like it aged, but—"

"Rob," Danielle said. "Don't bore the audience."

"Oh, he's not," Junie said. "I didn't even know water buffaloes made milk." Rob passed her another sliver of cheese from behind his side of the counter, and Junie popped it in her mouth.

Danielle smirked. "Well, there's more cheese where that came from, believe me," she said. "I'm gonna go outside and make a couple of phone calls. Rob, why don't you tell her more about the glorious world of buffalo milk?" Danielle whipped out her cell phone and left.

"Are you really curious?" Rob asked. He looked sheepish. "I mean, I know I could go on about it all day, but not every-one—"

"Tell me," Junie said, pulling up a stool from the corner of the store. She was the only customer there, and the room was warm and inviting. "I'm desperately in need of a cheese education."

Rob smiled shyly, as if he suspected she might be making fun of him. How was he to know she'd been daydreaming about him intermittently for the last week?

"Well," he said, "I guess the best thing to do is begin at the beginning. . . ." And then he launched into a comparative description of Italian cheeses, beginning with the familiar pecorino (sheep's milk), gorgonzola (cow), and romano (cow, almost always, although some farmers experimented with goat). Junie loved the sharpness of the cheeses, which Rob parceled out in thin slices. She concentrated on the contrast-ing textures and the deepness of the flavors. Rob gave her a handful of grapes to "cleanse the palate."

"So what else?" she asked.

"You want more?" Grinning like a kid at Christmas, Rob handed her samples of some of Piccolo Dairy's more esoteric offerings—taleggio, robiola, fontina, and mascarpone, which was sweet and creamy and tasted like cream cheese might taste in heaven. He told her of certain parmesans that cost hundreds of dollars a pound and of extinct cheeses that once were popular but that nobody could remember how to make.

"Did you know that some cheese is even illegal?" Rob said, clearly delighting in her cheese ignorance. The store was still empty of customers, but Rob brought his voice down to a conspiratorial whisper. "If a cheese is made with unpasteurized milk, it might have certain harmful bacteria in it, so it's illegal in this country. But unpasteurized cheese tastes different, sharper somehow—some people really love it—and I know these cheese freaks who smuggle it back in their suitcases from France and Italy. If they get busted, they're fined thousands of dollars."

"For smuggling cheese?"

"Yeah," Rob whispered, his eyes glinting. He was leaning on the other side of the counter, his head just a foot from hers. "And this is even better. In Sardinia, an island off of Italy, there's a famous sheep's milk cheese, a pecorino, that gets left out in the sun and infected with maggots."

"Oh, ew."

"It's true. It's called casu marzu—it means 'moving cheese' in the Sardinian dialect, and the maggots keep jumping till you swallow them."

"That is too disgusting." Junie laughed.

"I tried it once," Rob said. "It actually wasn't so bad. A little crunchy going down, though."

"You did not." Junie giggled. "You're crazy."

"Are you two still talking about cheese? How could you have anything left to say?" Danielle said, coming back into the store, her cell phone tucked into the front pocket of her jeans.

"Eat this and stop whining." Rob handed her a piece of pecorino. Just then a pair of older men walked into the store, smelling like cigars and dust. They wore dark felt fedoras and old-fashioned suits.

"Mr. Pirelli! Mr. Luprese! What can I do for you?" Rob asked.

"His best customers," Danielle said. "Let's get out of here and let my cousin sell cheese."

As they waited at the Broadway-Lafayette platform for the F train, loaded down with white paper packages of mozzarella and tagliatelle, Junie watched two mice running along the subway tracks. She was mentally toting up all the differences between Brian and Rob. Brian was tall and blond, Rob was dark and more compact. Brian listened to jam bands, Rob played opera in the store. Rob was a cheese guy. Brian was lactose intolerant. And, of course, Rob was probably at least twenty-one.

Junie looked down at the subway tracks. Did he even go to college?

"Why are you staring at those mice?" Danielle asked.

Junie was quiet for a moment before exclaiming: "I just don't know how it could work! I mean, we're so different! He's running a store, and I'm studying for the AP bio test!"

"Junie?" Danielle asked as the train rushed into the station, blowing their hair off their faces. "Try not to get melodramatic before you even go out on the first date, okay?"

Junie followed Danielle onto the train, clutching her bags. The warm salty taste of mozzarella was still on her lips.

The girls decided to have an impromptu dinner that Sunday night at Celia's house, mostly because Celia and Danielle had been assigned to complete part two of the interminable Shakespeare project, to design a stage set for the play.

"This assignment will never end," grumbled Danielle. "What do I know about set design?" She'd arrived with a massive antique *Collected Works of William Shakespeare* under her arms, which had been her mother's back when she attended St. Margaret's. Junie arrived with a bag of shrimp from Fish Tales, the seafood shop on Court: they were going to steam them, dump Old Bay seasoning on them (advice from the guy behind the counter, who tossed in a small can of Old Bay gratis), and eat them with their fingers. She'd passed Fish Tales on her way to Key Food and thought that shellfish might be a nice change.

Max and Jane were heading out in fancy clothes just as Danielle and Junie were heading in. They rendezvoused for a few minutes in the kitchen, where Junie put the bag of shrimp in a colander in the sink. "Celia's in her bedroom. I haven't seen her all day," Max said. "She's been working on something or other, Elizabethan set design, maybe? You must be Danielle. I've heard so much about you." He shook her hand warmly and complimented her on her small gold earrings.

Max seemed, Danielle thought, like a nice person, with the sort of manners her mother would consider "gentle-manly." He was enormous, though. Six and a half feet tall and built like a bear. The kind of guy who would seem threatening if you didn't know any better.

"You must be Jane, right?" Junie said to the blonde, who was inspecting her lipstick in the kitchen mirror.

"That I am, dear," she said. She patted at her sprayed hair and turned to the girls with a megawatt smile. "It is *so* lovely to meet Celia's friends."

"I don't know if he told you, but we hung out with your nephew the other night," Junie said. "He's really fun."

"Oh, isn't he adorable?" Jane beamed. "I just adore Henry. He's *heavenly*! And it was so wonderful of you girls to watch out for him while I stayed late at the gallery."

"We weren't really watching out for him," Junie said, but Jane was already distracted, sniffing the air like a terrier.

"What is that I smell? Is that . . . shellfish?"

"It's shrimp, Jane," Max said. "From Fish Tales, I'm guessing." He was a regular at all the neighborhood groceries.

"Does the smell bother you?" Junie took the shrimp out to rinse them in the sink, comfortable enough in Celia's house to simply show up and get to work.

"Of course not! Darlings, I *love* shellfish! Adore it!"

"The girls have been getting together to cook once a week or so," Max explained. He was getting some ceramic bowls down from the top shelf for Junie's shrimp. "It's almost like a dinner club."

"What a charming idea!" Jane exclaimed, clapping and standing next to Junie to inspect the shrimp. Max looked on with a bemused grin. That must be what he likes about Jane, Junie thought. She's so different from him.

"You know, Junie, I'm still waiting for my invitation to dinner," Max said, rubbing her head affectionately.

"Soon, Max," Junie said. "I promise."

"Tell that to Celia," Max said with a wistful sigh. "Jane, we better be heading out now. Leave these girls to their dinner."

"Good night, ladies!" Jane trilled. "Have a *fabulous* evening!"

"Good night," Junie and Danielle said. As the door closed behind Max and Jane, they stared at each other in horror.

"She gone?" Celia stuck her head into the kitchen.

"She's gone," Junie said. "Dear God."

"I know," Celia said. "And my father's like totally in love with her. I've never seen him like this, such a puppy dog."

"She's so—hair-sprayed," Danielle said. "With all the 'fabulous' this and 'charming' that."

"What did I tell you?" Celia got a lemon out of the fridge for the shrimp.

"It's weird," Junie said. "She's really not the least bit like her nephew."

Celia just shrugged. "They're both short."

"Henry's not *that* short," Junie said. "He's just a little shorter than you, Cee."

"What's your problem with Henry, anyway?" Danielle asked. "He seemed like a cool guy."

"Didn't he strike you as sort of full of himself?"

"Not really," Danielle said.

"I thought he was nice," Junie added.

Celia took a sponge and began wiping down the kitchen table. "Well, I guess Henry's not as bad as I first thought," she said, clearly choosing her words with care. "I mean, it's nice that he's adventurous, and he can be interesting to talk to. But he's so overbearing. And he has the most horrible taste in music."

"I think Ninja Star might be good after a few more listens," Danielle said.

Celia and Junie both shook their heads slowly: no way.

Dinner was quick and dirty this time—shrimp shells on the floor and Old Bay seasoning staining their hands and stuck under their nails. The shrimp was delicious, tasting of summer and the seashore. It reminded Junie that it was almost May already, and in a month the school year would be drawing to a close.

"Thank God this project isn't due until next week," Danielle said, wiping her red-stained hands delicately on a paper towel. "My hands are too messy to design a set."

Junie ripped off the shell of a pale pink shrimp and popped it in her mouth. She had the tallest pile of shells next to her plate and an arrangement of crumpled paper towels on her lap, translucent with grease. After every fourth shrimp she took a swig of ginger beer.

"Hey, Danielle, have you seen Steve lately?" Celia asked.

"Don't even mention his name." Danielle groaned. She was having the most trouble with the shrimp, unable to completely rid them of their shells; in fact, she seemed vaguely grossed out by the whole proceeding. "He totally disappeared. I've been calling him all weekend and he's nowhere."

"Are you nervous?" Junie asked. "About what he's up to?"

"Nervous? Nah, I'm sure he's just working on some new songs or something. He's got a show coming up in a few weeks, and he sometimes gets really intense before shows, working on his music." Danielle picked up another shrimp, but it slipped out of her fingers. "Junie, what are you doing next Saturday morning?" Danielle asked, changing the subject.

"I have track until eleven—why?"

"Well, it's Mrs. Lucci's birthday, and there's a party in the neighborhood, and I think Rob's coming. So I was figuring, if you weren't doing anything . . ."

"I'm so there."

"I thought you might be," Danielle said, ripping the head off a slippery shrimp.

Grouper, Sea Bass, and Penguins

Come Monday, Steve Reese was still nowhere to be found, and Danielle didn't feel quite as blasé about the situation as she'd pretended to be the night before. Steve wasn't picking up the phone in his apartment, his cell had been disconnected, and Shrub said he hadn't seen him in two days. Danielle tried the Coffee Carriage, but the girl behind the counter just shook her head when Danielle asked if she'd seen him. "That loser never showed up today. I have to work overtime to cover for him. Irresponsible jerk."

Danielle felt herself deflate. "Was he here yesterday?"

"I don't know. I don't work Sundays."

"Is there anyone I could ask?"

"No. Listen, I don't know anything, I told you," but then the girl caught the expression on Danielle's face and softened. "If I see him today, I'll tell him to call you. What's your name?"

"Danielle. I'm his girlfriend."

"You are?" The girl gave her a funny look. "His girlfriend?"

"Something wrong with that?"

"No! No." She shrugged. "Whatever. If I see him, I'll tell him to call his . . . girlfriend."

When Danielle got home, she pounded up the stairs and slammed the door, turned Jay-Z's "99 Problems" up loud, and started to scream along—her favorite form of stress relief. She closed her eyes and tried to scream away the humiliation, the rage, the condescending look on the Coffee Carriage counter girl's face. She shook her hair around and jumped up and down and used her stuffed monkey as a microphone. She had no idea anyone was home.

"Danielle! For Christ's sake! *Could you please turn that awful noise down?*"

"What?" She opened her eyes. Christina was at her door, wearing a bathrobe, her head wrapped in a towel. Danielle turned down the music. "Shouldn't you be at work?"

"Half day," Christina said. "Shouldn't you be at school?"

"It's four-thirty," Danielle said, dropping the stuffed monkey.

"Right," Christina said, starting to leave Danielle's doorway, but then she turned back around. "Just so you know, you're gonna ruin your voice if you scream like that." She was using her usual I'm-older-and-I-know-best voice.

"Christina, why should I care about ruining my voice?"

"Because I still have hopes you're going to use it someday instead of only singing at home in the shower."

"Whatever," Danielle said, tying her hair back in a ponytail.

Christina was one of the few people in the world who knew the real reason Danielle refused to sing in public. Back when the Battaglias used to attend St. Martin of the Piers, Danielle wanted nothing more than to join the famous church choir. She had daydreamed about it since she was a kid, took lessons with Mrs. Kim in Park Slope just to get her voice ready for auditions. Listening to the choir was the reason Danielle loved church: the glorious harmonies, the a cappella beauty of the voices. Sure, the choir was all male, and sure, it was the most award-winning church choir in Brooklyn, but eleven-year-old Danielle felt confident that if the priests just heard her sing, they'd let her join. She was the best singer her junior high had ever had, after all. How could they not?

Three days after her twelfth birthday the church held its annual auditions, and Danielle was ready. She put on her new patent leather shoes, carefully braided her hair, and borrowed her mother's favorite pearl bracelet. Nonna held her hand and together they walked to St. Martin's, ready to make history. But the priests in charge didn't let her sing a single note. Instead the scowling Father Joseph said, "Proper young ladies don't sing in public, especially not in all-male choirs."

Father Pierre added, "I think it takes a certain nerve even showing up for auditions for an all-male choir."

And Father William added, "And hasn't your father left the family home, young lady? Girls whose fathers have left are often trouble, and we don't want troubled girls—"

"Or any girls—"

"That's right, or any girls, in our award-winning choir."

Humiliated, Danielle stood on the stage, stared down at her new shoes, and forced herself not to let the priests see her cry.

Nonna had never been quite so furious. Cursing St. Martin's to anyone who would listen, she broke fifty years of Battaglia tradition and moved her family to Sacred Heart–St. Stephen on Carroll Street, a warm, loving church with a coed choir. But Danielle didn't audition for the St. Stephen choir. In fact, she refused to sing in public ever again.

No matter what her family said.

"So are you just standing there for your health, Christina? Do you have anything else to say?"

Christina shook her head. "Nothing you want to hear," she said, closing her sister's bedroom door.

As Celia was running out the door Tuesday morning, the phone rang. Max was already at the studio—maybe he'd left something at home he wanted her to drop off?

"Yeah?"

"Celia." A deep, British-accented voice. A quarter to eight in the morning. Henry must be out of his mind.

"What do *you* want?"

"Hello to you too, love. I was thinking that since our Williamsburg adventure was such a success, perhaps I could convince you to come to Coney Island with me today."

"Coney Island? Are you insane? I have school, Henry."

"So skip it," Henry said. "Take a risk. I bet you've never skipped school before."

He was right. She hadn't. And frankly, the thought of sitting through such a beautiful day in musty, overheated St. Margaret's broke her heart. Still, why would she skip to spend the day with *Henry* of all people?

"Come on, Celia," he said. "School will still be there tomorrow."

Outside, the birds were chirping and a warm breeze blew. It was undeniably a perfect morning for strolling by the water, not for wrestling with cosines and work equals force times distance. "I can't believe I'm even considering this," she said.

"Don't consider it," Henry said. "Just say yes."

Oh, what the hell. She was already pissing off her father. What did she have to lose?

Celia met Henry at ten o'clock at the Coffee Carriage, where he bought them corn muffins and lattes to go. He was wearing his electric orange windbreaker and khaki cargo pants, and his black hair flopped into his eyes. His ever-present headphones hugged his neck. For a second Celia was glad to see him, before she remembered how annoying he could be.

"I still can't believe I agreed to this," she said. She'd left a message with the school secretary saying she had a stomach bug and wouldn't be in today.

"It'll be fun," he said, biting into his muffin. "Usually it's just me stumbling around with no idea where I'm going. It'll be good to have someone else alongside me to deflect the attention."

Coney Island was at the very end of the F train, a collection of rotting souvenir shops and fast-food stands on a ramshackle boardwalk that stretched out beside the beach. The Astroland amusement park still stood along the eastern end of the boardwalk, but its amusements were decaying and empty. Nevertheless, the day was sunny and warm, so Celia and Henry walked quietly down the pier. She was surprised at how easy it was to slip into comfortable silence.

When they hit the New York Aquarium, a low-slung building at the end of the strip, Henry asked, "Shall we?"

Celia had nothing against fish. "Sure."

Inside, the aquarium was cool and dark and, because it was a weekday, pretty empty. A few groups of docile school-children were led around in pairs, but Henry and Celia ducked them and headed over to the three-story central tank, where leopard sharks, stingrays, groupers, hammerhead sharks, and schools of sea bass floated serenely past. Watching the fish swim in steady, fluid rows was even better than meditation.

Periodically a grouper would turn to them and gaze at their faces through the tank, its enormous fishy lips blowing kisses at them, its fins waving back and forth. It was an ugly fish, big and bulge headed and a gloomy midnight blue color. But when it turned its face toward them, it was also kind of cute.

"Do you think they like living here?" Celia asked. "I mean, do you think they'd rather be out in the sea, where they could swim wherever they wanted?"

"I'm not sure," Henry said. Secretly Celia liked the way his accent glided over words, the way his *r*'s disappeared and his vowels sounded much deeper and more important. "I suppose it's not too terrible here, really, insulated from the bad weather and the predators. On the other hand, perhaps it gets boring just swimming in the same circles your entire life. But on still another hand, who knows if fish have any concept of boring?"

"That's three hands." Celia smiled.

"So it is."

The grouper turned away from them and joined its fellow groupers swimming past. "Come on," Celia said. "Let's go visit the penguins."

Outside, in a rocky enclosure, the short, pudgy penguins marched around barking and nudging, waddling belly first on top of the fake cliffs until they dove into the penguin pool to swim as gracefully as any of the fish. Although they were black and white and two feet tall, there was something almost human about their chatter and gait, and Henry did a not-too-terrible penguin impersonation, holding his arms stiffly at his sides and turning his feet out. The crowd of first graders standing near them burst into appreciative laughter.

"Watch me!" one of them yelled, bowleggedly imitating Henry imitating the penguins.

"Me!" shrieked another one, breaking into a Charlie Chaplin strut.

"Come on, guys," said their teacher, a pretty young woman with a poofier afro than Celia's. "Let's leave this nice couple alone."

"No, no, we're not a—" Celia said, attempting to correct the teacher, but she wasn't listening, too busy concentrating on her students. "We're not a couple," Celia muttered to herself.

At the marine mammal exhibit Celia and Henry waved to the walruses and looked out at the Coney Island view. "It's funny what you'll do as a tourist. I've lived in London all my life and never visited the London Aquarium. The thought of it never even crossed my mind. But here I am in New York, acting utterly touristy."

"Well, when I visit London, I'll probably act all touristy too."

"You have plans to come to London, then?" He turned his big brown eyes to her.

"Not specifically," Celia said, staring at the walruses in their pen, trying to ignore the unexpected butterflies in her stomach. "But someday I'd like to check it out."

Behind them, a sea lion barked. Suddenly, unexpectedly, Celia wished Henry would lean over and kiss her. Oh God, what was happening to her? She pressed a hand against her cheek to make sure she wasn't feverish.

"Something wrong, love?" Henry asked.

"I'm fine," Celia said, in a sterner voice than she'd intended. "Stop calling me love."

But instead of looking offended, Henry just nudged her shoulder and winked.

La Bouche was a gourmet store in Brooklyn Heights that Junie's parents sometimes visited when they were in town, coming home with olive bread and cheeses wrapped in grape leaves. Tuesday evening, after track practice, Junie took the subway to the store and poked around, trying to seem invisible. Quietly she surveyed the selection of crackers and cookies, which was much more glamorous than the display at Piccolo Dairy. Here cheeses were festooned with red and green ribbons and wrapped in straw, and terrines were laid out behind glass and decorated with flowers.

"May I help you?" asked the woman behind the counter.

"I was interested in, um, cheese," Junie said. "I mean, I was interested in finding out about—" Suddenly she felt like an idiot. She'd wanted to research Rob's favorite topic and impress him when she saw him at Mrs. Lucci's party, but casually, so that they'd be talking and she could be all, "Oh, I had a really good cheddar the other day," and he could be like, "Tell me about it," and then she really could. But in the abstract, without Rob there to remind her that cheese could be cool, the whole idea seemed moronic. What kind of high school junior cared that much about cheese?

"Sure," the woman said. "What kind would you like to try? We have a lovely brie here, imported from France."

"Actually," Junie mumbled, "I was curious. Do you guys have any mozzarella di bufala?"

"Buffalo milk mozzarella?" the woman said. "I'm afraid not, dear. It's possible you could find some in Manhattan, but I suppose it would have to be specially ordered from Italy."

"Is that true?" Junie asked.

"It is, I'm afraid," she said. "Are you sure I couldn't get you some brie?"

Junie felt a perverse swell of pride at her association with

Rob's rare mozzarella. Satisfied, she shook her head, thanked the woman, and left.

During Wednesday's endless English class—a slide show of Elizabethan theaters, as if they comprised something more than plank floors, thatched roofs, and stadium seating— Danielle slipped out and checked her cell phone messages. She'd left one for Steve saying that if he didn't call her by 11 A.M., she was going to hunt him down and kill him.

"And shouldn't we be in class, Danielle?" Sister Frances had snuck up behind her, a prunish old lady who started every sentence with a conjunction: *but, so, for, and.*

"Sorry, Sister Frances. I just had to check on something—family emergency."

"But cell phones aren't permitted on campus, dear." Sister Frances's face twisted into a sinister smile. The sister was in charge of the select school choir and was forever up Danielle's butt trying to get her to join. "So I'm sure you'll want to leave yours at home, where it belongs."

"I told you, I have a *family emergency,*" Danielle growled. "I need it."

"Is there something we could help you with, dear? Parental concerns? Health issues? For of course we are here for you outside the classroom, too." Her eyes were twinkling, and Danielle knew she was thinking about select school choir.

"No, I mean, thanks, but it's nothing like that." Danielle scratched her knee.

"So then why don't you hand me your cell phone, dear,

and I'll make sure you receive it after the school day ends."

Danielle kept scratching. Oh, how she couldn't wait to graduate from St. Margaret's and say good-bye forever to its itchy skirts and squadrons of miserable nuns. "I'm sorry, Sister Frances, but I can't," she said, and then turned purposefully and marched down the tiled hall and out the school's carved wooden doors. Sister Frances called after her the whole time. "Danielle Battaglia! Danielle Battaglia! Don't make me call your mother!"

Oh, go ahead, call my mother, you sex-starved troll. Good luck getting through the Macy's switchboard.

As Danielle flew down Montague Street, the catcalls started from the local construction crews—that St. Margaret's uniform did it every time. How ironic that the nuns would dress me up like Britney Spears, she thought, kicking a stray beer can on the sidewalk.

Ducking into the vestibule of a bookstore, she dialed Steve's number at home. No luck. She then tried his cell, just in case it had been reconnected. She then thought about calling information for the number at the Coffee Carriage but decided it would be easier to just walk there, so she took off her stupid St. Margaret's vest and untucked her blouse—she'd have to go back to school at the end of the day to retrieve her book bag—and headed south on Court Street toward the coffee shop.

And there he was. Outside, smoking a cigarette, watching the traffic pass like he'd been standing there all his life. Even though she was mad at him for disappearing, for a moment

Danielle's stomach still knotted with joy at the sight of him—how dark his eyes were, how chiseled his arms, how perfectly his jeans hugged his ass.

"Where the hell have you been?"

"Hey, baby," Steve said lazily, taking a drag off the cigarette. He extended his arm to touch her waist, but she shifted out of his reach. "How's it going?"

"Steve, for the past five days you've been totally missing in action! I've searched for you everywhere—your apartment, here, around the neighborhood—I asked Derek, I asked Shrub. . . ." Danielle realized she was sounding hysterical, so she took a deep breath.

"I'm sorry," Steve said. He took a final drag and then mashed the cigarette out under his shoe. "I've been holed up trying to finish some new songs, you know? I think I've really got this new sound down, less guitars, less heavy on the bass, more vocally access—"

"Steve, *where have you been?*"

He smiled at her like the Cheshire cat—profound and indecipherable. Then he turned his head away and lit another cigarette.

"Steve, come on, don't make me freak out again, please?"

"You remember Skye?" he asked. "She's decided to rejoin the band. I've been working on the new stuff with her at her place."

Danielle's heart plummeted into her stomach. "By working on new songs," she asked, "do you mean having sex?"

"Baby." Steve was doing his best to look wounded, but he

131

couldn't make the Cheshire cat smile disappear completely. "If I said I was working on songs, I was working on songs, all right? I don't know why you have to get all possessive on me."

"Possessive?" Danielle shrieked. "Maybe because the last time you told me not to get possessive, I found out you were doing Angie Forenza? Maybe because you've been gone without a word for the past five days? Maybe I wouldn't get so *possessive*, Steve, if you weren't such a jerk."

"Danielle," Steve said. "You're freaking out."

"I am not."

He sighed and flicked his cigarette across the street. "You know I care about you, don't you? Why would I spend so much time with you if I didn't care about you?"

"Don't pull this, Steve." Inside, she could hear Nonna's voice: Be careful, *bambina*.

"Come on, Danielle, it's true. You know I want to be with you. Even when I can't be with you, I'm thinking about you. Don't you remember 'Good Danielle'?"

"Of course I do," Danielle said. She hated the weakness in her voice, but oh, how she wanted to believe him.

He reached out to touch the back of her neck and this time she let him. "Jesus, Steve," she whispered. "Why do you have to be so impossible?"

"Oh, baby," he said, rubbing the back of her neck with his strong fingers. "What Skye and I have is just music. What you and I have is so much more than that. We understand each other." He leaned into her, and she could smell his delicious smell: sweat and cigarettes and coffee.

"And you're not having sex with Skye?" Danielle asked, her rage slipping away, almost against her will.

"Oh, man, of course not." Steve pressed her up against the brick wall of the Coffee Carriage and kissed her there, long and slow and wonderful. Whatever. He could disappear when he wanted. As long as he kept kissing her like that, everything was forgiven.

Keys,
Rumors,
and
Tragedy

Celia was lighting the lavender candles in the living room when she heard a key turn in the lock. Max was home early, which seemed strange because he'd been so frantic finishing his sculptures for next week's gallery opening. As far as Celia knew, he hadn't found out about her day off from school— she figured that the nuns didn't call to check on her because she'd never given them a reason to suspect her in the past. As far as the sisters knew, she was just studious, polite, artsy Celia Clarke. If she said she was sick, she was sick.

Celia took off her sandals and gently placed them to the right of *Dying Pig*. She heard the door open and close, but her father knew better than to disturb her while she was meditating. She closed her eyes and assumed her meditative pose.

"Hellooo? Anybody hoo-oome?" What was Jane doing here?

"Jane, I'm in the living room," Celia said, struggling out of the baddha konasana position. Keys! Max had actually given her *keys*!

"Oh, hello there, darling! I'm sorry to disturb you—are you in the midst of your little meditation? Your father told me how important it is that you get your ten minutes of deep breathing every day."

"You have a key to the apartment now?"

"Oh, don't look so *violated*, darling!" Jane tinkled. "I'm just doing some inventory here for the gallery, trying to figure out what we should ship to the Upper East Side and what's going to stay. What do you think about the pig, dear? Stay or go?"

Celia put her shoes back on. "The pig's part of the family."

"Then he'll stay." Jane was holding a clipboard; she was dressed in one of those matching velour sweat suits, this one a perfect Barbie pink. Her hair was twisted in a complicated bun on top of her head. "But I think I'm going to ask Max if he's willing to part with *Burning Branches*. That one's a certain sale. I know at least ten clients who are just going to *adore* that piece."

"I always liked *Burning Branches*," Celia said. The sculpture consisted of three narrow steel rods, welded together at one end and tipped in brass.

"So will the public, darling." Jane scribbled a few notes on her clipboard. "You know, I was here yesterday afternoon doing some cataloging while your father was at his studio."

"Is that right?"

135

"The phone rang, you know. Ordinarily I wouldn't *dream* of picking up the phone in another person's home, but I was concerned that it might be Max trying to get in touch with me. I had left my cell phone at the gallery, you see."

"I see," Celia said, blowing out the candles and not really listening.

Jane scribbled something else on her clipboard. "So anyway, it turned out that it wasn't Max at all, but a certain Sister Mary Sebastian."

Celia froze. Jane didn't look up from the clipboard. "The poor sister was hoping that her favorite student's stomach flu wasn't too miserable and was curious to know whether or not she'd be back in class today. In fact, I believe she was hoping to speak to you." Jane raised a single eyebrow but continued to scribble.

Christ. "Look, Jane, it's not like I usually ditch—"

"But I told the good sister that while you were at the moment fast asleep, you were expecting a full recovery."

Celia let it sink in: Jane had gotten her off the hook. "You said that?" she said, floored with gratefulness.

Jane looked up at her then, smiling, her eyebrow still raised. "Henry told me he had a glorious time with you at the aquarium, darling."

He did? A glorious time? Celia bit her lip in order not to smile.

"I decided that in the interests of your burgeoning career as a tour guide, it would be best not to tell your father about your little bout with the stomach flu."

Celia gulped. "That's really nice of you, Jane. Thanks."

"No worries, dear. Now, which do you think would be better in the show, *Untitled Four* or *Scarlet Night*?"

"I mean it. It was nice."

"Enough. Tell me which sculpture you prefer for the show."

"*Scarlet Night.*"

"My thoughts exactly."

The rumor had taken a while to start moving, but by Friday it had spread like a virus around the Brooklyn Prep campus. Now, as Junie and Amanda sat in AP history, waiting for Mr. Applebaum to start class, Junie tried to figure out what was true and what was just gossip. According to Maggie McGee, who'd heard from Dave Weissbaum, who'd heard from Dan Cho, who was *there* when it happened, Amanda Begosian had had sex with Brian Cooper at Richard Langer's party on Friday night, the one that Junie hadn't been invited to.

"Amanda," she said, in between nervous coughs. "Answer me." But Amanda refused to either confirm or deny.

Sex with Brian! *Junie's* Brian! Could that even be possible? It wasn't that Amanda and Junie were best friends, but they were definitely close enough so that this sort of behavior counted as wildly uncool. Lab partners, track teammates, definite social acquaintances, for God's sake! How could she do this? And inside, Junie was kicking herself, because she'd always known that sweaty, stupid Amanda had a thing for Brian.

"I'm just saying," Amanda said, "that whatever happened

was a total accident and it's not going to happen again." She had circles under her eyes and a sad expression on her face. Her blond hair, usually carefully straightened, was pulled back in a sloppy ponytail.

"Amanda, just tell me. I promise I won't get mad."

"You already said that."

"So why won't you tell me?"

"Because you don't need to know."

There was nothing that infuriated Junie more than condescension. The fact that Amanda, her erstwhile friend, might or might not have had sex with her ex-boyfriend was actually not as disgusting to Junie as the fact that she refused to tell her. What the hell did that mean, "You don't need to know"? Of course she needed to know! *Brian was her ex-boyfriend!*

She was considering leaning over and throttling Amanda when Mr. Applebaum started in: "Robert E. Lee graduated second in his class from the United States Military Academy in 1829. He received no demerits as a student, which is an achievement that has yet to be repeated in the one hundred sixty years since Lee graduated. . . ."

Junie opened her notebook and began scribbling: *Lee, U.S. Military Academy, no demerits, second in his class, go to hell Amanda Begosian . . .*

About halfway through the class, as Robert E. Lee was beginning his 1845 slog between Mexico and the United States, Amanda put a piece of paper on Junie's desk. Junie looked questioningly over at her, but she refused to raise her eyes. Junie opened the note slowly. It read, *Yes, we did it, but only because we got really drunk. I'm so sorry, Junie. I've regretted it every second since it happened and I hope you can find a way to forgive me. If you can't, though, I understand.*

Oh, this was just perfect.

Junie's throat burned with anger. How could they! Those JERKS! But then, a second later, she was then filled with a sudden, almost schizophrenic calm. Why shouldn't Amanda have sex with Brian? After all, somebody should probably sleep with the poor guy. And besides, she had Rob now—or at least she had plans to have Rob.

But then the rage returned. Amanda, slimy little gossipy Amanda, drink-all-night-and-run-all-day Amanda . . . If he had to screw someone, couldn't Brian at least have found somebody a little more interesting?

Amanda looked up at Junie, and her cheeks were red and splotchy. "I'm sorry," she mouthed.

Junie looked down at the note again and then back up at Amanda. Brian really didn't love her anymore. He had slept with someone else.

It hurt more than she would have expected.

"Can you forgive me?" Amanda whispered.

Junie shrugged, crumpled up the note, and turned back to Mr. Applebaum to listen to the long, boring story of Robert E. Lee. She blinked several times in succession, refusing to let Amanda see the tears welling in her eyes.

"I never liked that girl," Celia said. Celia had a tendency to get jealous of Junie's Brooklyn Prep friends, as though Junie could ever love a new friend as much as she loved Cee, whom she considered closer than a sister. "She always seemed a little stuck-up."

"She's not really stuck-up," Junie said. "She's just kind of sweaty."

They were at the bodega on Carroll Street, buying flowers to bring to Nonna. Tonight's dinner was at Danielle's house, and both Junie and Celia were excited for the feast Nonna had promised them: pork with mustard sauce, stewed wild mushrooms, and more of Nonna's famous tiramisu.

"I just can't believe she had the nerve to sleep with Brian." Celia dug a bunch of pink roses from a bin and handed them to Junie. "It's a rule that your friends can't sleep with your ex-boyfriends. Everybody knows that. Even *I* know that, and I've never even *had* an ex-boyfriend."

"I can't talk about it anymore. All day it's been playing in my head like some kind of disgusting porno—Amanda doing Brian, Brian doing Amanda."

"Okay, just stop, you're grossing me out," Celia said. "I really don't need the visuals."

"Sorry." Junie paid for Nonna's pink roses and stuck her wallet into her jeans. "Danielle's going to freak out when I tell her."

But they never got a chance to tell her. When they arrived at the house on Fourth Place, Danielle opened the front door pale and tear streaked. They could hear women crying behind her.

"Danielle? Are you okay?" Junie asked, clutching hard at the flowers.

Danielle shook her head. Whoever was crying behind her started crying even harder.

"Danielle, what's going on?" Celia asked, reaching out to touch Danielle's arm.

"Nonna," Danielle whispered. "She died this afternoon. Massive heart attack. Three o'clock."

"Oh, Jesus, I'm so sorry," Junie said, and reached out to touch her new friend, wrap her in a hug. Celia came forward and did the same. For a few minutes the three girls stood on Danielle's front stoop and held each other while inside, the Battaglia women cried.

Cigarettes, Moonlight, and Chocolate Cake

The funeral was that Saturday at Scotto's funeral parlor on Court Street, across from the grocery store where Nonna used to buy milk, next to the sewing shop where she used to find fabric, and down the street from the bakery where she used to order pastries. Her entire life had taken place in the space of these few blocks. So it was fitting that she should be mourned there, too.

Inside Scotto's, a somber man greeted Nonna's family and friends and directed them to a small room off the lobby, all red velvet and heavy curtains and dark wooden pews. In the front, Nonna lay peacefully in her mahogany coffin, her eyes closed, her hands folded across her chest. She was wearing a black dress and a small gold crucifix around her neck. Someone had tucked a rose at her side.

"I guess it's not that gross," Junie whispered to Celia. Neither girl had ever been to a funeral before, and they hadn't known exactly what to expect. Celia had imagined something sort of waxy; Junie had been thinking more *Night of the Living Dead.* "She looks kind of peaceful."

"I wonder if she knew she was dying," Celia said. "Or if it was just like one second she was wiping the counter and the next minute she was out."

"I just hope it wasn't painful," Junie said, turning away from the open coffin. "She was such a nice lady. I really felt at home around her."

"I know," Celia said. "Danielle was so lucky to grow up with all these women around her. It's like she had three mothers."

"Three mothers who really loved her."

"Girls, girls, hello . . ." It was Rita, who had come up behind them and put a hand on each shoulder. "Thank you both so much for being here."

Junie didn't know what she was supposed to do—hug Rita? Shake her hand?—but Celia pulled it together immediately, wrapping Rita in a firm hug. Rita was pale and red eyed, but she had taken the time to have her hair done, and it fell in neat waves around her face. Smudged eyeliner rimmed her eyes. "It was so unexpected, you know?" she said after Celia let her go. "I'm on the phone with her, and the next thing I know she's making these strange noises. . . . I hung up with her and called the ambulance and then I rushed right home. But—but by the time I got there, she was gone. Thank God for Danielle."

"Danielle was there?"

"Held her hand the entire way to the hospital. Was by her

side when she passed on." Rita wiped her eyes and sniffled into a tissue. "She's so strong, my girl."

"Rita!" called an old lady standing in the corner. "Oh, *mia ragazza povera! Vostra madre povera!*"

"Mrs. Rocatello!" Rita cried, drifting toward her with her arms extended to be held in another sorrowful embrace.

Danielle was standing in a group at the side of the room, surrounded by old ladies in black dresses who pinched her chin and stroked her hair and kissed her cheeks. Christina was beside her, getting similar treatment. Junie recognized one of the women as Mrs. Lucci, although every single old lady looked pretty much the same: graying curls, black dresses, orthopedic shoes.

Sunshine flooded the dark room for a moment as a guest walked in the door. It was Rob, somber and unbelievably handsome in a navy suit.

"Stop staring," Celia said.

Junie blushed.

When the priest came forward to address the crowd, Danielle slipped away from the old ladies and grabbed Junie and Celia's arms to pull them with her to the front row. Danielle sat down in between Junie and Rita, and Junie instinctively took her hand. It was sweaty and cold.

"Friends, we are gathered here today to mourn Maria Luisa Bollino, mother of Rita and Salvatore, may he rest in peace, grandmother of Christina and Danielle, who today has joined her dear husband, Arturo, in heaven, under the watchful eyes of our Lord."

The priest had a deep, rumbling voice. He was balding,

but he had a five o'clock shadow, and he wore round, rimless glasses and a heavy gold ring.

"Maria Bollino was a fixture in this community. She could remember everybody in the neighborhood: whose grandchildren had been baptized, who was serving overseas, who was having surgery, who was celebrating an anniversary. Her Christmas cookies were famous from Fourth Place to DeGraw. With her death, Maria leaves an entire community bereft, for I know I will miss seeing her each Sunday, sitting in that fourth pew over there, with her beloved daughter, Rita, who . . ."

Just then something caught in Junie's throat. She cleared her throat to push it away, but it stayed there—tickling so bad she wanted to explode in a fire burst of coughing. She pressed her fist to her mouth and tried to ignore it.

"Go get some water," Celia whispered from her other side.

"But it's rude to get up—" And here she coughed.

So Junie stood and, attempting to remain as inconspicuous as possible, tiptoed out to the lobby and then outside the building, where she leaned against a wall and coughed and coughed. Oh, the dread spontaneous coughing fit—and always at the most awkward moments. Like during funerals.

"You okay?" Rob was standing outside, rubbing out a cigarette butt with the tip of his shoe. In his suit, in the bright sunshine, he looked like a movie star.

"What?" Junie said, wishing he'd caught her at a slightly sexier moment. "Oh yeah, I'm fine. Unexplained, uh, coughing fiasco, but nothing terrible." She inhaled and exhaled to regulate her breathing. She inhaled again. "You smoke?"

"Sometimes," he said. "At funerals."

"Right," Junie said.

"I know it's a bad habit."

"There are worse ones," Junie said. Now that she was done coughing, she considered asking him for a cigarette just to have an excuse to stand outside with him for a few more minutes. But the truth was, she thought smoking was gross. "I'm sorry about Nonna," she said.

"Me too," Rob said, putting his hands in his pockets. "She was an incredible lady. And she didn't have such an easy life, either. Lost her son, her marriage had its ups and downs, her daughter's marriage fell apart . . ."

"She was your father's aunt, right?"

"Yeah. But she looked after him like a mother, especially after his own mother died. My father's a wreck right now."

"Did he have other aunts and uncles?"

"No. Which is one of the reasons they were so close." He looked straight at Junie then and she felt some kind of electric flash between them, a kind of oh-what-I'd-like-to-do-to-you-right-now spark.

"I'm sorry for him," she mumbled, afraid that she was blushing. God, what kind of idiot gets turned on at a funeral? "I mean, you know, my thoughts are with the whole family."

"Thanks," Rob said, and took a step closer to her, like maybe he was thinking about hugging her because hugging was what you did at funerals.

Just then Junie noticed a big flake of ash that had settled

on his dark suit. She leaned forward to pick it off his lapel. As soon as she stood near him, she felt enveloped in a kind of tingly warmth.

"I'm sorry," she said. "You just had this ash on your—" He put his hand on hers. It was warm and his skin was tough, calloused. Were they going to hug now? She looked up.

And in one of those completely unpredictable, breathless moments, he leaned down, put his lips on hers, and kissed her. His lips were soft and warm. His tongue touched hers gently. "My God," Junie whispered.

"I know," Rob said.

A second later they were pressed against the brick funeral home wall, kissing furiously. The nicotine on his breath tasted weird, dirty and delicious at the same time. Junie ran her hand through his dark curls. He kissed the side of her neck and her chin. She rested her fingers on the smooth skin on the back of his neck. He kissed her collarbone and traced his fingers down her bra strap. It was only when a passing car honked at them that Junie pulled away.

"Rob, we can't do this at Nonna's funeral," she said, adjusting her ponytail. Her heart was pounding wildly, and she could feel the goose bumps on her arms.

"You're probably right." He was grinning, but so casually that Junie wondered if making out at funerals was a regular thing for him. He straightened his tie. "Let's go back in."

Junie wiped the saliva off her lips and attempted to still her heart. Add another one to the list, she thought. Williamsburg Phil and now Rob. Mrs. Finnegan would flip out.

They hurried through the velvet-swagged lobby and

stood together in the back of the funeral chamber, close enough to hear each other breathe. The priest had finished speaking and was sitting in a corner of the room; Danielle was now standing at the podium. She was wearing a long gray dress, her hair was pulled back, and a large gold cross hung around her neck, just like Christina's and Rita's.

Thank God, Junie thought, she hadn't missed her friend's eulogy.

Danielle placed her hands on the lectern and exchanged a nervous nod with someone in the audience. Then she opened her mouth and, instead of delivering a speech, sang the most chillingly beautiful rendition of "Ave Maria" that Junie had ever heard.

Ave Maria
Gratia plena
Maria, gratia plena
Maria, gratia plena

When she was done, the mourners sat silent for an entire minute. "Wow," somebody said under his breath. Danielle bowed her head and sat back down. From the back of the room Junie stared at her, awestruck.

That night, missing Nonna, Danielle visited her grandmother's room, thinking about how she would have loved to hear her "Ave Maria." After the whole St. Martin's fiasco, Nonna never pressured Danielle to join a choir or anything stupid like that. She just got very quiet when Danielle sang around the house, closing her eyes and whispering along. Sometimes Danielle would sing extra loud in the living room if she knew that Nonna was in the kitchen, listening.

Danielle sighed and felt her eyes blur with tears. Wiping them away with the edge of her T-shirt, she took a good look around Nonna's room. On her grandmother's bureau there was a black-and-white photo of two frowning people in turn-of-the-century clothes. Nonna's parents? She picked it up and looked at it closely. These people were stern looking, thin lipped, but there was a hint of Nonna's twinkle in both their eyes. How come Danielle had never seen this picture before?

Opening a drawer, she wondered what else Nonna stored away in this room. It didn't feel like she was snooping; it felt like she was honoring Nonna somehow, paying attention to the things she never bothered to notice while her grandmother was alive.

There were photo albums of Danielle's mother and her dead uncle Salvatore when they were babies, with special notations about how much they weighed at birth, who their godparents were, when they each took their first steps. Even as a kid, Danielle's mother wasn't pretty—she was chubby and awkward and sort of greasy looking. Uncle Salvatore, on the other hand, had been really handsome. His hair rose off his head in an Elvis Presley–style pompadour, and his blue eyes sparkled. In another album Nonna kept Uncle Salvatore's dog tags and all the letters he'd sent home from Vietnam before he was killed.

Nonna kept her modest selection of jewelry in a small cherrywood box on her dresser. She had a jumbo crucifix, two cross necklaces—one with a diamond in the center—a pair of pearl earrings, and the ruby engagement ring she stopped wearing once her hands started to swell with arthritis. She had a cameo brooch and another brooch with an enamel flower on it and, hidden under that, a pin that Danielle had made for her when she was in the first grade, a paper sunflower with the words *World's Best Nonna* written on it in careful first-grade handwriting.

In her top drawer Nonna had kept a surprising collection of lacy lingerie, most of it at least thirty years old and cut for a much slimmer, perkier woman than the grandmother Danielle had known. "Nonna!" she exclaimed out loud, holding up a see-through black lace nightgown. "Damn, woman!"

Under the lingerie was a packet of letters wrapped in pink ribbon. Danielle untied them, trying to be careful with the flimsy, ancient paper under her hands. They were addressed to Arturo Bollino, the grandfather she'd never met. They were all dated from the 1950s: 1953, 1957, 1959. And they were all written on frilly pink paper and signed by a woman named "Lydia."

Arturo, the first one began. *My heart aches for you as I write this. At work I cannot concentrate, for I can only think of your lips kissing my lips, the sweet dark curls of your hair.*

What the hell was this?

My sweet Arturo, read the next one. *Oh, what I would give to see you again, if only for an hour, but how much better for a whole night!*

Arturo, my angel, my darling. It is such torture not to be near you now, for while I sleep next to my husband every night, my dreams are only of you.

Arturo, it kills me to love one man and yet be married to

another. And while I do not wish for you to hurt Maria, how can I not long to be with you?

Oh my God!

Danielle could feel her eyes bulging from their sockets. Her saintly grandfather, "Arturo, rest his soul, your blessed grandfather," was a philanderer! *And Nonna knew about it!* The questions rocketed through Danielle's brain as she held her grandfather's letters with shaking hands. How did Nonna find these letters? Who the hell was this Lydia person? And why did Nonna continue to talk about her dead husband as if he was some kind of angel if he cheated on her throughout the 1950s? *"While I do not wish for you to hurt Maria, how can I not long to be with you?"*

Her grandfather had been a lying, cheating, gigantic creep.

She wondered if her mother knew. Should she tell her? Or should she keep this to herself? But how could she keep this to herself? Carefully Danielle retied the letters and then collapsed onto her grandmother's bed. So this was why Nonna had always warned her to be careful about men. She knew what kinds of jackasses they could be.

She had the proof hidden in her lingerie drawer.

Danielle found her mother in the dining room, eating a piece of chocolate cake and gazing at the portrait of Salvatore. "Mrs. Lucci insisted on coming over and cleaning the house," she said, not taking her eyes from the portrait. "She and Mrs. Rocatello mopped the kitchen, crying the whole time." She paused and put down her fork. "You sang beautifully this morning."

151

"Thanks, Mom." Danielle sat down next to her mother and pinched off a piece of cake with her fingers. "How are you holding up?"

"Oh, okay, I guess. I mean, I miss her already, but I guess I feel better than I did yesterday."

Rita ate another bite of cake and then wiped her mouth delicately. "You know, she had a good life. She had the exact life she wanted. Friends, family, grandchildren she adored. And she died without illness. She was always afraid of that, some long debilitating illness. So I guess she did all right in the end." Rita sighed. "I'm going to miss her, though."

"I will too," Danielle said. Should she tell her mom about Lydia? Should she ask her if she knew?

"I like to think she's with Pop now," Rita said. "That's what makes me happy."

"Hey, Mom? Nonna and your father—they loved each other, right? I mean, as far as you could tell."

Rita looked at Danielle curiously. "Well, they had their ups and downs like anybody else, but I think at the end of the day they loved each other. My father was a good man. It's a shame you never met him."

"So they were happy?"

"I guess so. Why?"

Danielle thought for a second, and then she thought again. She leaned over and kissed her mother on the cheek. "Oh, nothing. I'm going to take a nap, Ma."

"Okay. I think I'll take one too. All this grief is exhausting."

Danielle and Rita climbed the stairs to their respective bedrooms, neither one saying another word.

*　　*　　*

At four-thirty in the morning Celia's cell phone began buzzing. She ignored it, but a few minutes later it began to buzz again, wildly. "What the—" She opened one eye and grabbed the phone off her nightstand.

"Celia? Are you awake? Wake up, love, wake up. . . ."

"Henry?" Celia rubbed her eyes and sat up in bed. "Why are you calling me this late? Are you okay?"

"I'm right outside," he said. "Look out your window."

Celia parted her curtains and looked down onto Bergen Street. There stood Henry at a pay phone, waving at her. His hair was slicked back and he was wearing his neon windbreaker. He was smiling.

Celia's heart starting pounding. What in God's name was he doing here? She waved back. "I'll be right down."

She checked her hair, pulled her kimono over her pajamas, and tiptoed out of the apartment and down the stairs. Henry was waiting on her stoop, holding a cup of coffee in each hand. "Hello."

"Henry! It's four-thirty in the morning!"

"Already?" Henry shrugged. "I was clubbing, and I guess I lost track of time. I wanted some company." He rested against the railing for a second. "There's an all-hours deli around the corner that sells coffee," he said, handing her a paper cup. "I remembered that you like yours with sugar."

"Thanks." He wanted company? But weren't there other people at the club? Celia was stumped about how to handle this unexpected visit. She decided on casual conversation. "What band did you hear?"

153

"This Japanese group called Kudo. They're not nearly as good as Ninja Star."

"I find that," Celia said, "a little hard to believe."

They drank their coffee together in silence, Celia noticing, for the first time, what nice full lips Henry had. It was a clear night—the day's clouds had disappeared and the full moon hung heavily over the city. "Fancy a walk?" Henry asked.

Together they stood and walked down the street, saying nothing, drinking their coffee. The night air was cool and Celia pulled her kimono close around her. "You want my jacket?"

"I'm fine," she said.

They approached Smith Street, which was ghost-town quiet at four-thirty in the morning. This was the hour or so after the bars closed and before the diners opened—the air was still, empty, expectant. There was something magical about it. Celia allowed herself to glance at Henry, just as he was glancing at her. They passed the bodega, the hair salon, Scotto's funeral home, and then Carroll Gardens Park, whose swings and seesaws glimmered.

"Look at those two go at it, eh?" Henry said, gesturing with his coffee cup at a couple making out by the park's gate.

"Man, get a room," Celia said, stunned at their brazenness. They were practically getting naked in public! But there was something familiar about the guy, the tattoos on his arms, the dyed hair. . . . Oh no, Celia thought. Steve Reese. The only surprise was how unsurprising it was.

"Henry, I think that's the guy Danielle's been seeing," Celia said.

Henry shook his head. "But that isn't Danielle, is it?"

"No," Celia said, and before she knew exactly what she was doing, she was off, marching over to Steve, filled with disgust.

"Just what the hell is going on?" she asked, getting right up in their faces. She could feel her blood simmer. The pair stopped kissing and stared at her.

"What the—?" It was definitely Steve. He wiped his slobbery lips against his wrist. "Who the hell are you?"

"Who is this, Steve?" the girl asked. It was the redhead from the Coffee Carriage. The old singer from his band.

"I'm so sorry you don't remember me, Steve. I remember you." She turned to the redhead. "Did you know that Steve's been dating my friend Danielle?"

"He's finished with her," the girl said, adjusting her T-shirt.

"Not as far as she knows," Celia said.

"Excuse me, little girl," Steve spat. "Why don't you mind your own—"

"Did you know Danielle's grandmother died on Friday? Did you know that?" Celia got right in his face. "Did you know she's been asleep all weekend? That she's totally, completely depressed and the last thing she needs right now is a miserable loser like you making her life any worse?"

"Her grandmother died?" Steve asked feebly.

"That's right, you pathetic piece of garbage." Celia wiped her brow. "Go over there to her house tomorrow and pay your condolences. And leave this one"—here she pointed at the redhead with her thumb—"at home. Do you understand?"

Steve turned his head away.

"Tell me you understand, Steve."

"I get you." Steve looked up. "I get you."

"Good," Celia said. Then she marched off back across the street to where Henry was waiting for her, an extremely impressed look on his face.

"Man!" he said. "That was something. You got him crying out there! You cut his bollocks right off!"

"Well, that wasn't exactly my—"

"No, I mean it." Henry paused and grinned at her. "That was something. You're really quite incredible, Celia."

"Oh! Why, thank you, Henry," Celia said. Her cheeks remained red the whole way home—half in rage at Steve and half, she knew, in happiness at being with Henry.

Kielbasa and Ricotta

Sue Wong-Goldstein was in Warsaw this time, convening a meeting of angry Polish farming officials.

"So what's new?" Sue asked.

"Danielle's grandmother died."

"The one who taught you to cook? That's terrible. Was she sick?"

"No—a heart attack on the kitchen floor."

"My God," Sue said. Junie knew that one of her mother's greatest fears was of dropping dead on a plane somewhere, over one of the dozens of countries she was sick of traveling to.

"She was eighty-four years old, Mom."

"Still. Did you go the funeral? Was it okay?"

"Yeah, I went," Junie said, and could feel her heart pounding as though Rob were in the room with her. "It was . . . overwhelming. I mean, of course it was sad, but it wasn't—I don't know. How's the weather in Warsaw?"

"Terrible. You'd never know it's spring here—it's raining and fifty degrees. No wonder these farmers are in such bad moods all the time. However," Sue said, her voice brightening, "it's supposed to be eighty when I arrive in Rome. Anyway, I wanted to tell you that I'm coming home for your races next week. You're going to be in the Kings County meet, right?"

"You remembered?" Junie didn't mean to sound as surprised as she felt.

"Of course I remembered. It's right here in my PalmPilot. Kings County All-Track meet, May 4."

Junie couldn't remember the last finals her mother had attended. It had to have been six or seven years ago. What would it be like to have Sue in the stands? She'd stand apart from the usual collective of cheerleading parents, the Brenners, the Begosians, the Wheatleys, who stood together at every race and clapped for every runner. The Brenners, the Begosians, and the Wheatleys would have no idea who Sue Wong-Goldstein was.

"You know, I was thinking about it," Sue said, "and I realized that you'll be applying to college next year, and I won't have the opportunity to watch you run quite as often."

"That's true," Junie said. She felt oddly touched.

"Anyway, I have to get to a meeting, sweetie. The farmers are getting antsy. But I'll give you a call tomorrow."

"No problem, Mom. Eat some kielbasa for me."

"I already did."

It was seven in the morning, a grayish damp Monday, but Junie's spirits were sunny. First, her mother was going to come home to see her run. Second, Rob. All day yesterday she'd replayed making out with him in her head. Yesterday afternoon she'd stopped by Danielle's house with a bouquet of chrysanthemums, just to see how she was doing. She had to admit, though, that she was also hoping to catch Rob, in case he happened to be over. But Rob was at the store, and Danielle was fast asleep, said a weepy-looking Christina. She'd been sleeping all weekend. Nonna's death, Christina explained, had taken everybody's energy away.

Junie had left the chrysanthemums in a vase in the Battaglia foyer and left.

She was brushing her hair when the phone rang again. Probably Sue calling to tell her the Polish weather had changed. "Yeah?"

"Um, is this Junie?"

"Yes?" Junie said, her voice softer.

"This is Rob Prezza. From the other day. From Maria's, um, from the other—"

"Hey, Rob." Junie grinned.

"Is it too early to call? I thought you might be on your way to school and I wanted to catch you. I got your number from Danielle."

"It's not too early," Junie said. "It's fine. It's nice to hear from you."

"I was wondering what you were doing tonight," he said. "I mean, I know it's a Monday and you have school the next day, but I was thinking that maybe if you wanted, we could grab dinner together. The store closes at eight. You could meet me there."

She was charmed at how nervous he sounded. "That would be cool," she said.

"Do you remember where the store is?" And they traded cell phone numbers and directions.

"Great," Junie said. "I'm looking forward to it." She hung up the phone and a bright bubble of excitement burst inside her, and she smiled the whole way to school.

"So we have to tell her about Steve and Skye, right?" Celia asked. Monday afternoon Celia had come from school right to Junie's house to help her get ready for her date with Rob.

"Yeah, but it'll be hard. She's going through a tough time right now," Junie said. She had three different outfits spread out on her bed, but in the panicky hour before her date none of them seemed right. She wished she had cooler clothes: slinky skirts or funky T-shirts, the sort of stuff Celia liked to wear. She'd have borrowed some of Celia's clothes, except that her shirts and jeans were big enough for Junie to drown in.

"Wear the black pants," Celia said. "And maybe the striped button-down."

"I'll look too corporate."

"We'll punch it up. What's your footwear selection like?"

"Boring."

Celia sighed and shook her head. "Let's hit your mother's closet. Maybe she'll have something."

Fifteen minutes later Junie was dressed in a pair of black pants, a white tank, and her mother's pointy black flats. Celia was carefully painting eye shadow over her eyelids.

"So what are you going to do about Danielle?" Junie asked.

"Right, right. I think she should know, of course. But then again, how do I hit her with this so soon after her grandmother died?"

"But I don't think it's fair of you to keep it a secret," Junie said. "I'd hate it if you had privileged information that you didn't tell me—especially if it was about a guy I was seeing. Remember how mad I got about Amanda Begosian? And Brian and I had already broken up."

"True," Celia said. "But on the other hand, timing is everything."

Junie shrugged and slipped on one of her mother's black cardigans. "You know, you never mentioned why Henry showed up at your house in the first place."

"I don't know." Celia shrugged. "He said he wanted company. It's not," she added, defensively, "like I'd invited him or anything."

"He wanted company at four-thirty in the morning?"

Celia busied herself folding discarded T-shirts. "He'd been clubbing. Anyway, we just took a walk. It was no big deal."

"Cee, it's okay if you like this guy," Junie said gently. "Nobody's judging you."

"Who said I liked him?"

"I'm not saying you do, necessarily," Junie said, rubbing some gel in her hair. "It's just that if you *did* like him, you know you could tell me. I'm your best friend, Cee. You can tell me anything."

Cee nodded and opened Junie's jewelry box, fumbling through the tangle of beaded necklaces and silver bracelets.

It was clear that she was struggling with something, but it was just as clear she didn't feel like talking about it. Fine. Junie knew Celia well enough to know when to give her time. "Look," Celia said finally. "We're not here to talk about Henry, we're here to talk about Steve."

"Of course, I know."

"So are we gonna tell Danielle what we saw or not?" She was suddenly all business.

"Of course we are," Junie said. "Soon. We can't keep her in the dark. And if you don't want to mention you were out walking with Henry, I certainly won't mention it either."

Celia rolled her eyes. "I told you, *this is not about Henry!*"

"I know," Junie said. She'd better drop it. Celia found a lipstick in a dark shade of red and applied it to Junie's lips in silence. Junie closed her eyes, trying to put Steve and Danielle and Celia and Henry out of her mind and get excited about her date.

At seven-fifteen Junie took the F train to Piccolo Dairy. Rob was waiting outside when she got there, dressed in jeans and a long-sleeved T-shirt. His hair was wet.

"There's a shower in the back of the store," he said, kissing her hello on the cheek. "So I don't have to leave every day smelling like cheese. You look really nice."

"It's not so bad to smell like cheese," Junie said.

Rob laughed. "That's my girl."

They went to a Cuban restaurant on Elizabeth Street, which was surprising to Junie because for some reason she could only imagine Rob eating Italian food. When talking to the waitress, he busted out with fluent-sounding Spanish.

"You speak Spanish?"

"Only to impress the ladies." He grinned at her. Ladies? Fluent Spanish? Junie considered everything she didn't know about Rob's life. He must go out on dates all the time. He must have tons of girlfriends. After all, he was already in his twenties.

He ordered them lemon sodas (which was good, because Junie didn't want to deal with the whole to-drink-or-not-to-drink question) and chunks of corn smothered with paprika. "These are like little Cuban appetizers," he said. "They totally mess up your hands, but they taste really good."

Junie bit into one and immediately jammed some corn between her teeth. She tried to be discreet about removing it, but Rob caught her and smiled. He had some corn stuck in his teeth too. "This is the worst date food imaginable," he said with a laugh. "It's been a while since I've been out on a date. I guess I forgot."

Phew, Junie thought. He wasn't a player. She relaxed and bit into another piece of corn, teeth be damned. Her hands were turning red from the paprika. He was right—this was hideous date food.

"So what year are you in school, anyway?" Rob asked.

"I'm going to be a senior."

"Then you're a junior."

"Well, technically," she said. "But I'm trying to figure out where to go to college and stuff. I turned seventeen in March, though." Junie could hear herself sounding blustery. "Um, how old are you?"

"Twenty-one," Rob said. "I graduated from college a semester early."

"You went to college?"

"Of course," Rob said. "Are you surprised?"

"No, no, of course not. I just didn't, I mean I . . ." Junie could feel herself blush through her protests.

"It's all right." Rob laughed. "I went to NYU and worked in the store part-time. I was an English major."

"Really? That's what I want to be too. But my dad thinks I should study bio, go premed. He thinks it'll be better for my future."

"Well, English isn't the most practical major, but if you like to read, it's definitely the most fun. I studied creative writing, too."

"Are you a writer?" Junie asked as the waitress set down steaming plates of chicken with garlic, plantains, and rice and beans.

"Hmmm . . . not really. I have a couple of short stories that I've been working on whenever I have a day off, but that's not too often these days."

"Could I read them sometime?"

"You'd want to?" Rob asked.

"Sure," Junie said, taking a big, sweet, greasy bite of plantain. "I love to read, remember? Future English major." Secretly she was thrilled that he'd gone to college and that he had interests besides mozzarella.

"Well, just so you know, most of my stories are about cheese," Rob said, taking another bite of his rice and beans. She looked up to see if he was joking, but from the look on his face it was impossible to tell. She put down her fork. "Junie, I'm kidding."

"I knew that!"

"No." Rob laughed and threw a crumpled napkin at her. "You totally thought I was serious. That I go home at night to compose stories about ricotta."

"I'm sorry," Junie said, throwing the napkin back at him. "It's just that I've never met someone like you before."

"Someone like me?"

"You know, who runs a business and is an expert on a slightly weird subject—no offense—and who writes stories in his spare time."

"Well, I've never met anyone like you before, either. Someone who's so pretty, and who cares so much about her friends, and is willing to listen to me babble for hours." Rob looked down and then looked back up at her. "And someone who's such a good kisser."

"Aw, shucks," Junie said, her sarcasm masking her genuine embarrassment. An hour into their first date and she couldn't tell if Rob was cool or a colossal dork.

After they left the restaurant, Rob lit a cigarette.

"I thought you only smoked at funerals," Junie said.

"Among other places," Rob said, putting his lighter back in his jacket. "Does the smoke bother you? I'll put it out."

"No, it's fine," Junie said, but the truth was, between the cheesy lines and the smoking and the fact that Rob was four years older than she was—she wasn't turned off, exactly, but she was certainly a little more ambivalent than she'd felt pressed up against the funeral home wall.

165

It was a nice evening, so they walked from SoHo all the way up to Union Square. The conversation was easy and funny, but when they passed the Virgin Megastore, Junie saw that a new Phish album was hitting the stands, and she thought of Brian. Then Rob took her hand, and she turned her head away from the Phish poster. Rob's hand felt good— that was a good sign, wasn't it? Anyway, Brian wasn't hers anymore. Amanda Begosian had made that abundantly clear.

Eggplant
and
Betrayal

Rita and Christina were going back to work, so Danielle decided she should probably go back to school, too, even though she didn't feel like it. It was Tuesday, and they had taken the previous day off, sleeping and reading magazines and ordering in Chinese food. Last night her mother had suggested they go to the movies just to get their minds off things, and so even though they weren't really in the mood, they went to see a romantic comedy at the Court Street theater. During the movie they ate popcorn and drank Cokes, but they didn't laugh.

The St. Margaret's sisters all knew that Danielle had experienced "a tragic death in the family," and so they didn't give her the usual hard time when she failed to pay proper attention in class. Celia met her at lunch with corn muffins from the Coffee Carriage, and Sheila Lynn Daly gave her a big hug in between classes, even though she and Sheila Lynn weren't particularly close. Danielle just drifted through school, thinking about her grandmother and all the things she'd never known about her. All the things Nonna had been too proud, or too strong, or too something to ever tell.

In English class Celia passed her a note proposing an impromptu girls' dinner at her house. *Come around seven,* the note said. *We can bake brownies and just chill.* Danielle passed back a note agreeing; it would be good to get out of the house.

In math class Mrs. Brown, one of the civilian teachers, told her not to worry about missing Monday's quiz. She could make it up whenever she felt like it, maybe next week sometime. "Thank you, Mrs. Brown," Danielle murmured, trying to forget that on a normal day Mrs. Brown could be such an uptight pain in the ass.

Finally three o'clock came. Danielle collected her books at her locker even more quickly than usual, but as she was trying to escape out the school's back door, Sister Frances caught her by the sleeve. "I too heard about the tragic death of your grandmother, Danielle. So I want to offer my condolences."

"Thank you, Sister," Danielle mumbled. Oh, how she wanted to get out of there.

"You know, dear," Sister Frances said, "sometimes when one is in mourning, it feels good to open one's mouth and sing. Singing is a way we can connect ourselves with those who came before us. With the spirits who roam this world."

"Okay, Sister Frances."

"It's just a suggestion, Danielle." Sister Frances pressed

two fingers against her heart. "Peace be with you, my child."

"And peace be with you," Danielle said. The sister released her arm, and Danielle bolted out of there and practically ran for home. The sister would never understand. Danielle would never sing in any kind of school group, choir, musical, sing-along, or Christmas pageant chorale. She'd made that promise to herself, and she wasn't going to break that promise just to make some crusty nun happy.

Back on Fourth Place, wearing sweatpants, Danielle parked herself in front of the television to watch MTV and eat leftover funeral food. Cold eggplant parmigiana and sausages and peppers, with a hunk of semolina bread balanced at the edge of the plate. At first, after Nonna died, she'd had no appetite, but in the past few days she'd become ravenous. She picked up a pepper and ate it with her hands, wondering exactly how it was that Nonna's sausages and peppers tasted so right and Mrs. Lucci's tasted so off. Surely the two women used the same ingredients, the same methods: fry the peppers with onions and garlic in a splash of olive oil, wait till the onions start to soften, add the sausages, a pinch of salt, and a couple of shakes of pepper, and that was basically it. Mrs. Lucci's version, which was what Danielle was eating now, was decent but nowhere near as delicious as Nonna's.

The doorbell rang. Probably another flower delivery. Danielle wiped her hands on her sweatpants and opened the front door.

"Hey, baby."

"Steve?" He looked terrible: tired and pale, his hair limp, his lips chapped. "What's wrong with you?"

"I'm so sorry, Danielle," he said. "I just wanted to tell you that."

"Thanks, Steve. I appreciate it. I'll tell my family." It was strange, she thought, but in the past few days she'd basically forgotten Steve even existed. But she was really glad he was here right now. Maybe he'd want some leftover eggplant?

"No, I'm not just sorry about your grandmother," he said. "I'm sorry about Skye. About everything."

"Steve, what are you talking about?"

He looked stricken. He rubbed his left eye with his index finger. "Didn't your friend tell you?"

"What friend? Tell me what?"

"The tall girl, the black one with the crazy outfits. About the other night."

"What about the other night?" But inside, Danielle knew what must have happened. Celia must have seen Steve out with Skye somewhere. *And she hadn't said anything.*

"Ah, come on, Danielle. Don't make me spell it out."

"Spell out what?"

"I mean . . . everything your friend saw—"

Everything your friend saw! How could Celia not say anything? Weren't they supposed to be friends? Or was this girls' dinner thing all some sort of garbage, some let's use Danielle for her cooking skills but not tell her when we catch her man cheating on her kind of garbage?

"You know what, Steve? I've had a tough couple of days. I mean a *really* tough couple of days. And so I don't have the energy to yell at you." Danielle took a deep breath. She was so weary. "So if you could just get off my porch and never bother me again, I think we could call it even."

"But Danielle—"

Please, Steve, go away. Just go away. Please. "Steve, I'm tired," she said. He nodded at her and took a step back so that she could close the door in his face.

Danielle didn't feel like leaving the house, but she was too mad at Celia to stay still. How dare that girl see Steve and Skye and not tell her? She'd had more than two days to open her mouth and she hadn't said a word! She *knew* how important Steve was to her. She knew all about their history. Why would she keep it a secret? If, Danielle fumed, she caught Celia's boyfriend cheating on her, she'd march on over to Celia's house and tell her right away. Right away! That's what you did when you caught a man misbehaving. *You told.*

Danielle felt her eyes start to water. So here's where she stood: first she lost her grandmother, and then she lost Steve, and now she was losing her friends. What had she done to deserve all this?

She threw on her sneakers and ran over to the community center, where Celia was teaching a class. The community center was a squat brick building on a block halfway between Carroll Gardens and Park Slope; inside, it was neatly tiled and cheerful and scrubbed looking, like a swanky private school. She checked with the guard to see where Celia's class was.

"Upstairs, sweetheart," the guard said, half winking, but Danielle was in no mood.

"Where upstairs?"

"Room 205. Wipe that frown off your face, girl! It can't be that bad!" But Danielle was already bounding up the wide stone stairs to the second floor. She stopped in front of a glass door that looked in on a bunch of girls in tights, turning somersaults across a series of dark green mats. Celia was helping a fat one curl up into a ball. She looked so professional in the classroom, so trustworthy, wearing loose yoga pants and a bright scarf around her head. Not treacherous in the least. What a great actress.

Fifteen minutes later the class was over. Danielle waited for the little girls to file out of the room before pouncing.

"So when were you going to tell me that you caught Steve cheating on me? Or were you just planning on keeping your little secret to yourself?"

"Excuse me?" Celia looked startled and clutched her gym bag.

"Don't act like you don't know what I'm talking about. He came by my house this afternoon and told me what you saw."

Celia touched her scarf as if for reassurance. "God, Danielle, I was planning on telling you about it tonight, but I didn't want to freak you out so soon after your grandmother died."

"If you catch someone's boyfriend cheating, you tell them right away! Everybody knows that! You just don't sit around and wait for the perfect moment! There's no such thing as a perfect moment!" And suddenly Danielle flashed back to a memory she'd half forgotten: the look on her mother's face when she found out that Danielle's father had been running around on her. Pain was etched all over it but so too was the wretched humiliation of realizing that everybody in the neighborhood already knew.

"I didn't realize," Celia said, "that there was a statute of limitations."

"Maybe if you'd ever had a boyfriend, you'd have known."

"I'm going to ignore that comment," Celia said, bending down to get her bag. Danielle could see she was desperate to keep her face composed. Her lips were pressed hard together.

"I thought you were my friend, Celia."

"I am your friend. So please, I'm begging you to calm down. Listen—"

"Don't tell me to calm down!" Danielle struggled to keep control of her voice. "Don't patronize me. I don't need your protection. You're not my mother and you're not my sister and *you're not my grandmother.*"

"Danielle—" Celia's eyes opened wide.

"Friends are supposed to be honest with each other. And you weren't honest with me at a time when I really needed my friends." And for the first time since Nonna died, Danielle felt herself start to bawl. She really hated crying, especially in front of other people. So she turned around and hurried out of the community center, ignoring Celia, who was shouting after her.

As soon as Celia finished making sure each of her girls had been handed over to a parent, she packed up her books and headed for Junie's house. She was still in shock over what Danielle had said to her. Patronize? Lie? Celia had never meant to hide anything or be dishonest in any way. She had never wanted to hurt Danielle. Why would she? Danielle was one of the very few friends she had in the world. Of course, these days it seemed like Celia was good at alienating the people she cared about most. She and her father, for instance, hadn't had a real conversation in weeks.

Junie wasn't home yet from track, so Celia sat on her stoop and took out her copy of *Much Ado About Nothing*. Much ado about nothing—exactly what was happening between her and Danielle. She looked down at act two of the play, where Claudio says, "Friendship is constant in all other things / Save in the office and affairs of love."

Once again, Celia thought, Shakespeare knew the deal.

"What are you doing here? I thought we were meeting at your house tonight." Junie bounced up her stoop, still sweaty from track practice, a big duffel bag over her shoulder.

"No dinner tonight," Celia said darkly. "Or maybe ever again."

"What are you talking about?"

"Danielle came to the community center to flip out at me for not telling her about Steve and Skye."

"Oh my God," Junie said, dropping her duffel bag. "How'd she find out?"

"I guess Steve showed up at her house and told her." Celia bit her lip. She felt faintly nauseated.

"Did you tell Danielle that we were going to explain it all to her tonight?"

"I tried. But she was mad that I'd known for this long and hadn't said anything. She called me 'patronizing.'"

"Wow," Junie said, sitting down on the stoop next to Celia.

"I know. It really sucks." Celia rested her chin in her hands. Why did relationships have to be so confusing? All she wanted in life was peace of mind and harmony with the world. Get up, get dressed, go to school, come home, study, meditate, sleep. In between laugh with your friends, eat some good food, read some good books, help the planet a little. Celia's goals were simple. Why did the world have to complicate them?

Across the street a young father was showing his daughter how to ride a bicycle. He held her steady as she started down the sidewalk, but every time he let go of her handlebars, she started to wobble dangerously. Watching the two of them made Celia feel a tiny bit better. She admired the little girl's determination to keep trying.

"So what should I do?" she said after a minute.

"Danielle needs us right now, even if she doesn't know it," Junie said thoughtfully. "And you've got to explain to her that you never meant to upset her."

"I know," Celia said. "I just hope she believes me."

Across the street the father let go of his little girl's bicycle, and she managed to stay balanced by herself. Junie clapped, Celia gave her a thumbs-up, and the little girl gave them both a big freckled smile.

"Hey, why don't we just make dinner and bring it over to Danielle's house?" Junie proposed. "See what she says?"

"I guess it's worth a shot." Celia closed her eyes and

leaned back against the stoop. "I mean, right now I really have nothing to lose."

Back when Celia was a little girl, her father used to make a dish specifically for times when they missed her mother the most. Max called it "heartbreak stew," even though it was, in essence, just tuna noodle casserole with some curry powder tossed in. Evidently Celia's mother hadn't been much of a cook, and this was the only dish she made that usually turned out pretty good. For a year after her death Max couldn't so much as look at a can of tuna, but on the first anniversary of that terrible car accident, he made himself and Cee a batch of heartbreak stew. It seemed like the right thing to bring to a grieving family. It had always seemed to help Max.

Junie showered while the noodles boiled, and Celia grated cheddar cheese into a bowl and crunched some stale cornflakes into crumbs. She had put on one of Junie's father's Bill Withers CDs, and sang along halfheartedly to "Ain't No Sunshine" as she buttered a Pyrex casserole dish.

"Feeling any better?" Junie came down the stairs, her hair damp, wearing her usual corduroys. For a second Celia envied her friend. Junie didn't have to strive for simplicity and calm; she simply seemed to embody it. She ran long-distance track. She got good grades. She wore plain clothes and a long black ponytail and never had to worry about being the tallest girl in school with the kinkiest hair and the darkest skin. Even though her parents traveled a lot, they were both still alive, and they doted on her. Sometimes it seemed like Junie's biggest problem was which cute guy to make out with—the cute boyfriend, the friend's cute cousin, the cute guy up on the roof.

Junie wrung out her ponytail over the sink. "You okay, Cee?"

"I'm cool," Celia said. She tried to remind herself that from other people's points of view, her own life would look pretty good right now too. It was all a matter of perspective. And suddenly she wondered where Henry was.

Heartbreak stew was easy to make. Sauté some mushrooms in butter, add flour, stir in the grated cheddar and curry powder and mix all that up with the boiled noodles. Add two cans of tuna, pour the whole mess into the buttered pan, and pour some melted butter over that. Spread the cornflakes on top.

"Smells good," Junie said after the casserole had been in the oven for twenty minutes. She'd never eaten heartbreak stew before.

They wrapped the casserole in aluminum foil and then in clean dish towels to keep the heat in. They walked the twelve blocks to Danielle's house quickly, holding the casserole upright like waiters bearing a tray.

Danielle opened the door with an unkind look on her face. "What do you two want?"

Neither Junie nor Celia said anything for a second. "Dinner?" Junie finally squeaked.

"Sorry, guys, but I'm not in the mood," Danielle said, and tried to shut the door, but Celia stuck her foot out to stop it from closing on them.

"Look, Danielle," she said, taking a deep breath, "I know

you're mad at me for keeping secrets from you, but I promise I never meant to hurt you. I was just waiting for the right time to tell you about what I'd seen. And I know what it's like to be hurt, and I know what it's like to grieve, but we made this dinner for you 'cause we thought it would make you forget for a while about being sad and grieving."

Danielle didn't say anything, just stared at them. She reached down to scratch her knee.

"Anyway," Celia continued after a few awkward seconds, "we're supposed to do dinner tonight and frankly that's my favorite part of the week and I don't want to miss it. And I really don't want us to fight."

Danielle kept scratching at her knee, as if deciding something. Finally she turned around and walked into the house, but she left the door open so that Junie and Celia could follow.

They ate the heartbreak stew and white bean salad and stewed tomatoes with basil that Mrs. Lucci had dropped off that morning. Rita and Christina came home from Macy's and poured each of the girls a little red wine from the carafe they kept on the counter. Then they sat down and joined the girls at the dining room table, and the five women ate somberly but well at the old wood table.

Rita had heard about Rob's date with Junie. "He was very excited," she said. "Rob's dad called me up to tell me. Rob talked about you all day today."

"We had a good time," Junie said simply, hoping she wasn't going to start to blush.

"I don't think Rob's dated anybody seriously since Debbie from school," Christina said. "He's pretty picky."

"What did you two end up doing?" Danielle asked.

"Dinner at some Cuban place," Junie said. "And then we took a walk around Union Square. It was really fun."

"Cuban place?" Christina asked. "Did he try to show off his Spanish?"

"Totally," Junie said. That was it. She was blushing. Yet underneath her blush she felt a bit guilty that she wasn't 100 percent sure about Rob. She didn't know why she wasn't—he was so cute and friendly, and he seemed like he was into her. But there was something just a little weird about him, even beyond the cheese. Or maybe she just wasn't ready to start dating someone new?

Rita, Christina, and Danielle were beaming at Junie like she was a new member of the family. Junie ducked her head and took another bite of white bean salad.

After dinner Celia and Junie stuck around to help clean up while Christina went out to take a walk and Rita settled down in front of the television. "It was so sweet of you girls to help out," Rita said before disappearing into the living room. "You've both been so good to us."

"It's our pleasure," Junie said.

Celia began to wrap up the leftovers. She had been quiet throughout dinner, as though her speech at the front door had used up all the words she had for the night. Whatever tension the dinner had eased slowly began to return, filling the kitchen with silence.

"Look, I'm sorry I freaked out at you," Danielle finally

said. She was drying the dishes that Junie was washing. "I just felt so frustrated, like all these things were spiraling out of my control. I didn't mean to take it out on you. I shouldn't have. I'm really sorry."

Celia looked up. She had a sponge in her hand. Please, Junie thought. Please say you're over it. Celia could bear a grudge sometimes. "That's okay," Celia said after a long pause, much to Junie's relief. "I'm sorry too. I should have told you about Steve immediately."

"No, I understand what you were trying to do. I know you didn't mean to keep anything from me. And anyway, in the end I'm kind of glad it happened. It's time for me to get losers like Steve out of my life for good."

"For good?" Junie asked.

Danielle shrugged. "I think it's what Nonna would have wanted." For the second time that day, she started to tear up a little. Junie came over and put her arms around Danielle. She was little but strong, and her arms felt really comforting. In a moment Celia joined them, and the three stood in the middle of the kitchen, hugging.

"You're my girls," Danielle whispered.

"It's true," Junie said.

"Preach it," Celia said.

And they stood there hugging as the clock ticked past two more minutes and it was time to finish cleaning up.

Iced Tea,
Picasso,
and
Apartment 20B

Celia got a text message during English class: *Have you seen Jane's apartment yet? It's worth a look if you haven't. Meet me after you're done with school: 337 East 86th Street, apartment 20B. H.*

She hadn't seen Henry in three days, and she knew that he'd soon be returning to London. She was glad that he wanted to see her, although deep down she was embarrassed at how badly she was starting to want to see him too. Two nights ago, when Junie asked her about Henry, Celia had wrestled with admitting it—but then just clammed up. She couldn't believe how vulnerable liking Henry made her feel. What if he thought she was too tall? What if he thought she was too dark? What if he thought she was too opinionated or too fierce or too . . . anything? What if he had a thing for blondes?

"Everything okay, Miss Clarke?" Sister Mary Sebastian

stopped in mid-rhapsody about the perfection of Shakespeare's sonnets.

"Couldn't be better, Sister," Celia said.

The sister raised her eyebrows. "Glad to hear it, Miss Clarke," she said.

Danielle was sitting on her other side. Celia had been nervous about seeing her today after all of last night's drama, but Danielle was chatty and cheerful, acting like nothing had ever happened between them. "What's the text?" she whispered.

Celia held up the phone behind her desk and showed her.

Danielle gave her a thumbs-up. Two minutes later she slid a piece of paper onto her desk. *You're gonna get some!* the note read.

Don't be disgusting, Celia wrote back.

After school Celia hopped on the 6 train and took it to the Upper East Side, home of her favorite museums, the Whitney and the Met, and her favorite stores: Barneys, Prada, Jimmy Choo. Sure, she could hardly afford to buy what these stores offered, but she could put her nose against the plate glass windows and dream.

Jane's apartment building was tall and fancy, with a doorman out front and a long, curving drive sweeping up to the double doors. The lobby was full of flowers. "I'm here for apartment 20B," Celia said to the man behind the lobby desk. "My name is Celia Clarke." She fumbled with her purse and tried to seem unassuming. Apartment buildings like these made her nervous.

"The left-hand elevator, ma'am. Apartment 20B is expecting you."

Upstairs, 20B was waiting for her at the door.

"You made it!"

"I made it," Celia agreed. She took off her jacket and looked around Jane's apartment. The place was small, and there wasn't very much furniture, but what there was seemed perfect and luxurious: a mahogany desk, a colorful rug. Even better was all the beautiful art that hung on the walls: a Warhol print in the front hall, two Cy Twombly canvases in the living room, and a red Calder mobile hanging over the dining room table.

"How did she manage to find all this stuff?" Celia asked, impressed.

"She's in the business," Henry said.

"But still. This artwork is pretty expensive and not so easy to find. Warhols and Calders . . . and is this a Picasso?" Framed in bright white, a pen-and-ink drawing of two birds hung proudly in the foyer. It was casually graceful, swift and fluid, clearly a Picasso, probably from the end of his career.

"It is," Henry said. "She got that drawing in London. It was a gift from his daughter's ex-husband. I think they used to date."

"Jane dated Picasso's daughter's ex-husband?" Celia tried not to sound too impressed.

"Years ago," Henry said. "Before she got it in her head that she wanted to move to the States."

He poured them glasses of iced tea and they went to hang out in Jane's living room: Celia on one couch and

Henry several feet away from her in an armchair. The uphol-stery was buttery leather, soft and pale yellow. Ginger, Jane's dog, paced nervously in the corner.

"So when are you going back to London, anyway?" Celia asked. She didn't want to know, but of course she did.

"Monday," Henry said. "I can't believe this trip is almost over. A month in New York, blam."

"What are you going to do with the rest of the summer?"

"I have a gig spinning at the club in Reading, starts the day after I get back home. And then maybe I'll travel with my mates to France at the end of the summer."

Boy mates or girl mates? Celia wondered.

"I guess it's the usual stuff," Henry said.

"It doesn't sound so usual to me," Celia said. By the time he gets to France, she thought, he probably won't remember me at all.

Henry shrugged. He was giving her an unusual look, a look she couldn't quite pinpoint. Celia stared down into her iced tea.

"Don't look so down, love," Henry said. "I'll send you a postcard."

"Sure, whatever." Celia stood up. Suddenly she felt irri-tated at the way Henry had been playing her for the past two weeks, showing up at her house in the middle of the night and then acting like he was her brother. She wondered if he knew how rare it was for her to like a boy, to actually like one enough that she'd consider getting with him. She wondered if he had any idea what a privileged position he held, being the first boy in her life to get a grip on her heart.

She got up and stared out the huge, west-facing window.

"Are you okay?" He stood behind her, all of Manhattan stretched out below them—the Upper East Side, Central Park, other tall buildings and skyscrapers and the city streets below. Down there, Celia thought, people were busy having lives. Men were kissing women. Women were being kissed.

"I'm fine," she said. But she wasn't, really. For the first time in her life Celia Clarke wanted something that she had no idea how to get. Henry bent down to scratch Ginger behind the ears. Celia watched, amazed to find herself jealous of a dog.

"I think I'd better go," she said.

"Are you sure? I thought maybe we could make dinner. I bought some curry powder yester—"

"No, really," Celia said, grabbing her book bag. "I've gotta bounce." And before Henry could stop her, Celia hurried out of the apartment toward the stairwell. It was twenty flights down, but she'd run all those stairs and more in order to escape her fear.

"Celia! Celia!" she could hear Henry calling after her. "Where are you going?"

Celia kicked off her heels and started to run.

Frappuccino, Apologies, and Tylenol

"Looking good!" called the guy on the corner of Smith and Baltic as Danielle crossed the street on her way home from school. She was sucking on a Frappuccino—she'd started going to Starbucks, encouraging everyone she knew to boycott the Coffee Carriage—and was in no mood for the whistling brigade that harassed her daily. "Hey, sexy! Why won't you come here and talk to me?"

Danielle glared at the jerk across the street but then softened when she saw who it was. Shrub, Steve's roommate. The vocalist in their band. "Shrub," Danielle called, walking toward him. "You should pick on girls your own size."

"What's up, sweetheart?" He gave her a peck on the cheek. "We haven't seen you around in a while."

"Oh, you know. Steve blew it again."

"That idiot."

Danielle smiled. She'd always liked Shrub—he was

funny and sweet, and he had a beautiful voice. He looked about ten years old, with bright red hair that stood up in cowlicks all over his head and freckles sprinkled across the bridge of his nose.

"He started cheating on me again, big surprise," she said. "With Skye, of all people. But you probably knew that."

"Oh, Stevie." Shrub shook his head. "Gotta have his hand in every pot."

"Ew, that's gross."

"You know what I mean." He grinned and crossed his eyes. "Anyway, Skye walked out on him. Hitched a ride to L.A. on Sunday without so much as a good-bye note. And now all of us are in trouble because we've got a show next week and no vocalist."

"What about you?"

"I can't sing those arrangements!" Shrub laughed. "You wanna hear me try and hit a high G? I'd puncture eardrums. Anyway, the lyrics are definitely girl."

"So what are you going to do?" Danielle asked.

"You got any ideas?"

Danielle sucked on her Frappuccino for a second as a thought gradually took shape in her mind. Singing at Nonna's funeral had changed things somehow. Performing "Ave Maria" in public had freed her from the memory of St. Martin of the Piers. And she knew what her grandmother would want her to do.

"Actually," she said to a puzzled-looking Shrub, "I do have an idea or two."

*   *   *

Junie was distracted throughout track practice and it showed. Finishing a third lap around the field, she tripped and fell flat on her face, her left knee bending awkwardly beneath her. The pain was agonizing. Junie squeezed her eyes shut and willed herself not to scream.

"Are you okay?" Amanda Begosian, who was still kissing Junie's ass in case Junie was still mad at her about Brian, stood over her, a worried look on her face.

"Help me up, would you?" Junie hated Amanda's pitying look.

"Sure, sure." She grabbed Junie's arm and helped her assume an upright position. But the pain inside Junie's knee felt like being stabbed by a hundred tiny pins, and she fell back down on her butt.

"I hurt my knee," Junie said flatly. "It's bad." She silently begged Amanda not to start talking about her own surgery last year. This was that injury. She could feel it.

Coach and the rest of her teammates swarmed around her. "You okay, Goldstein?" Coach asked, her suntanned face worried, the whistle that hung from her neck dangling in the breeze.

"I don't think so. Definitely a sprain at the very least."

"Oh no," Coach muttered. "Begosian, help her up and over to the trainer's office. The rest of you, give me four around the track."

Amanda, sweating violently, took Junie by the arm and helped her limp across the playing fields and over to the Brooklyn Prep sports building, the pride of the campus: a pile of bricks and plate glass with weight rooms, cardio rooms, two dance studios, and a pool. The trainer's office was on the ground floor, a nod to students with injured knees who couldn't make it up the stairs. There was somebody else in there with him, a baseball player making whimpering noises, so Amanda and Junie took a seat outside.

"Are you feeling okay?" Amanda asked, wiping her brow. It was the first thing either of them had said since Coach had sent them to the trainer.

"I guess. It only really hurts when I move."

"That's good," Amanda said, and then was quiet again. Junie counted the seconds until she brought it up.

"Listen, Junie—"

"I sort of don't want to talk about it, Amanda."

"Okay," she said, but Junie knew that she was going to mention it again. Five, four, three, two, one:

"Look, Junie, I'm so sorry. You have no idea how bad I've felt about everything that's happened. We were drunk, my resistance was down—and I just wasn't thinking. I wish I could take it back, but I can't. But I really wish you'd forgive me. I can't stand feeling guilty like this anymore."

Junie nodded, staring at the caricatures of the Brooklyn Prep sports heroes that lined the building's walls.

"I haven't even spoken to Brian since it happened. We both feel so bad—when we pass each other in the halls, we don't even talk."

"Yeah, well, Brian's good at that," Junie said.

"So are you going to be mad at me forever?" Amanda asked, and there was a note of exasperation in her voice. She was bouncing her leg anxiously up and down like a nervous child.

"No," Junie said, envying Amanda the movement in her leg. The truth was, since everything that had happened with Rob, Danielle, Celia, and Nonna, Junie hadn't spent too much time worrying about whatever Amanda and Brian had done one drunken night. It wasn't that she was trying to be particularly forgiving or mature about it, and it wasn't even that she'd stopped caring about Brian. It was just that since Brian and she had broken up mere weeks ago, so much else had happened.

"Do you still love him or what?" Amanda asked. Her leg continued bouncing wildly.

"I guess so," Junie said. "Sometimes." What she wanted to say was, *It's really none of your business,* but even though Amanda had slept with her ex-boyfriend, she couldn't bring herself to be rude. "Stop bouncing your leg."

"Sorry."

The baseball player dragged himself out of the trainer's office, holding his arm as tenderly as a newborn. The trainer poked his head out the door. "Who's next?"

After about five minutes and a series of painful pokes and twists, the verdict was announced: Junie had definitely sprained something, possibly even torn something, and would have to get herself to the orthopedic surgeon sooner rather than later. Her season was in essence over.

Amanda Begosian, still anxious to be helpful, generously offered to call a car to take Junie home. Only then, as she gave her address to the driver, did Junie remember her mother. Sue was flying home to watch her run in the finals. But there was no way Junie would be running next week or maybe even next season. She hoped her mother wouldn't be too annoyed that she'd exchanged a week with her European business partners for a week with her pathetic, invalid daughter.

Danielle had spent the afternoon with Shrub in the back room of the Rattletrap bar; she was allowed in despite her minor status because Shrub's older sister owned the place. Besides, she and Shrub weren't drinking. They weren't making out. They weren't even smoking up, despite Shrub's famous fondness for weed. "So what *were* you kids doing back there?" Shrub's sister asked as she got ready for the happy hour crowd. But neither Shrub nor Danielle would say.

When she got home, it was six o'clock and the house on Fourth Place was quiet. It was these times when she missed Nonna the most, these times when Nonna used to welcome her home with a hug and a glass of soda and sometimes a plate of spaghetti. Her soap operas or Mel Torme records would be turned up too loud, and her pale flowered house-dress would smell like garlic and onions.

Today, though, the only sound in the house was Tchaikovsky's *Nutcracker Suite,* which her mother liked to listen to year-round, even though to the rest of the world it was Christmas music. Danielle found her mother in the dining room, writing on white cards and putting them in envelopes.

"Whatcha doing?"

"Thank-you notes," Rita said. "I'm writing to all the people who came by after Nonna's death. Thanking them for the cards and the food and everything."

"Do you need help?" Danielle asked.

"I'd love some help, honey," Rita said, a bit surprised. So Danielle sat down across from her mother, took a pen from her backpack, and signed their names to the cards her mother had ordered. The cards read, *Thank you for your kind support during this difficult time.* Danielle and her mother had to fill out dozens of them. After a little while Danielle's wrist started to hurt, but still it was gratifying to sit there and think about just how much Nonna had been loved.

"You miss her right now?" Rita asked. She had put her pen down and was rubbing her wrist.

"I do," Danielle asked. Every day she'd been thinking about all those letters, tied up in ribbon in Nonna's drawer. She looked up now at the portrait of her grandfather. You ass, she thought.

"I miss her right now myself," Rita said. "'Cause I really don't feel like making dinner." She winked at Danielle and got up toward the kitchen, still rubbing her wrist. "Hamburger okay?"

"That would be great, Mom." While Rita cooked, Danielle scribbled. So many people had offered their condolences! The Caparis, the Rizzos, the Bergers, the Andresinis. Even Dr. Frank, the optometrist, even Mrs. Wang at the dry cleaners, had written notes to say how much they would miss seeing nice Mrs. Bollino around the neighborhood. Danielle finished scribbling just as Rita came back to the dining room with two plates of hamburgers on buns. Had Nonna been cooking, she would have made pasta with gravy and meatballs.

When Junie woke up from her nap her knee was red, swollen, and throbbing with a persistent beat. It was dark outside already, probably eight o'clock at least, and Junie considered planting her head back down on the pillow and going straight back to sleep. But she took another look at her leg; she needed ice. Somehow she managed to lift herself out of bed and then limped down the stairs, holding carefully to the banister, wincing each time she put any pressure on her leg.

At the first-floor landing she paused. It sounded like there were voices coming from the kitchen—two voices, a man's and a woman's. Could it be? She staggered down the hall, past the den, and into the kitchen. It was. Her mother and her father, drinking red wine in the kitchen. The entire Wong-Goldstein family, in the same place, at the same time.

"Hello? What are you guys doing here?"

"Princess!" Her father looked up and gave her a big smile. "Your mom and I both managed to get early flights in. You were sound asleep and I didn't want to wake you. Hard day at the office?"

"Oh my God, Junie, what happened to your knee?" Sue jumped up from the table and helped Junie to a chair. Her mother was still wearing a rumpled suit, and her passport was in her jacket pocket.

"I fell," Junie said. "At track."

"You need to see Dr. Rosenberg," Sue said. "I'll make you an appointment."

"Actually, Mom, I should probably go to an orthopedist, not a pediatrician. Could you just get me some ice?"

"Of course!" Junie decided not to remark on the weirdness of seeing both her parents at once. Suspiciously, she thought that mentioning it might take away the magic of it.

Sue sat down next to her and held the ice pack to her knee, which was looking more and more swollen by the second. Her father had already swung into action and was calling Dr. Rosenberg's answering service to get the name of a good orthopedist. Sue smiled at Junie, but Junie could see the exhaustion in her eyes. "I flew in from Rome this afternoon," she said apologetically. "It's the middle of the night for me."

"I'm not going to be able to run in next week's meet," Junie whispered. She squeezed her eyes shut; she felt flushed, slightly feverish. "I'm sorry I dragged you all the way here and I won't even run."

"Oh, sweetie pie, you didn't drag me," Sue said, reaching up to tuck Junie's hair behind her ear. "I missed you. I would have been here even if you didn't have the races."

Junie's knee still throbbed in a ticktock of pain, but at least she didn't have to feel guilty for dragging Sue all the way across the ocean for nothing. Her mother would have come anyway, or so she said, and that was a relief.

"Oh, by the way, someone called for you this afternoon," said her father as he hung up the phone. "A guy named Rob or Bob or something."

"Rob," Junie said, cringing as her mother pressed the ice to her knee. "What did he say?"

"He wants you to come by the store tomorrow. He said he got some new deliveries from Sicily."

"Who's Rob?" Sue asked.

"Oh, just this guy I know. He's my friend's cousin. The one whose grandmother died. Anyway, he has a cheese shop in Manhattan."

"Is this the friend who's been teaching you how to cook?"

"That's the one," Junie said. "She and Celia and I have been making dinner together once a week for the past month or so—Mom, could you not press so hard?"

"Speaking of," Ed said, "I could use some dinner right now. Anyone else starving?"

They all were, even Junie, whose knee was now throbbing but no longer looking quite as swollen. Unfortunately, she still couldn't stand up long enough to cook, and her parents didn't have the faintest idea what to do in the kitchen. So Ed picked up the phone again, and the Goldsteins relied on an old family specialty: Chinese takeout. Junie had an appetizer of extra-strength Tylenol.

Crutches, Grilled Cheese, and Fondue

Wednesday evening Celia and Danielle finally finished their set design project. Celia threw herself into it, sanding Popsicle sticks to use as the theater's floor and trimming the red velvet curtains with gold ribbons. Finally something to think about besides the ass she'd made of herself running from Jane's apartment. She touched brown paint onto the tiny proscenium.

"No wonder Sister Mary loves you so much," Danielle said, blowing on the glue that kept the theater's faux-thatched roof in place. "This theater is definitely nicer than anything from back in Shakespeare's day."

Celia grinned. She loved a job well done. She carefully wiped off the base of the set and left Danielle's house at twenty of eleven. She got home just in time.

Max was in the living room, wrapping some of his sculpture in moving blankets. The room looked awkward and bare: the couches pushed against the walls, the mobiles taken from the ceiling. "I made curfew," Celia said, trying not to sound bitter.

"It's ten fifty-six," Max said.

"So I made it," Celia said.

"So you did," he said. He carefully rolled *Scarlet Night* in layers of quilted plastic. Celia watched him for a second, waiting to see if he'd say anything else, but he stayed quiet.

Finally she couldn't take it anymore. "Dad, do we still have to be in this stupid stalemate?"

"Celia, that's as much up to you as it is to me," Max said. He put down the plastic-wrapped *Scarlet Night* and wiped his hands on his jeans. There was no anger in his eyes, only resignation. "Do you think I like fighting? Do you think I like it when you hide in your room instead of coming out to say hello? Do you think it makes me happy to piss you off with a curfew?" He shook his head. "None of this makes me happy, Celia. None of it."

"So then why are we acting like this?"

"You tell me," Max said.

Celia shrugged. She could list a dozen reasons: the early morning confrontation with Jane, the night she came back at two in the morning, all the times she taught another Yogilates class rather than come home and deal with her father. But she didn't want to focus on the bad stuff any-more. It was time to regain positivity.

"Look, Dad, if we put all that crap behind us, do you think we could try again? To be friends?"

"I'm willing to try if you are." And he looked up at her

and smiled, and she smiled back. It wasn't a perfect truce, exactly, but at least it was a start.

"What are you doing here, anyway?"

"Getting ready for the gallery show," Max said. "A moving company's coming to pick this stuff up tomorrow afternoon. Jane arranged it." He folded another blanket around *Burning Branches*.

"Cool," Celia said, and considered making her exit. Now that she and her father had reached some kind of peace deal, she didn't want to risk it by sticking around too long, giving both of them the opportunity to once again say things they didn't mean. But Max looked lonely by himself in the empty living room, and it had been a while since they'd spent time together. So Celia took another moving blanket over to *Four Friends*, a small steel blade with four lug nuts bolted up its side. Max looked at her, nodded, and returned to his work. For a while they worked in silence, quiet and methodical. As she wrapped, Celia took time to admire her father's sculpture. It really was so well crafted, forceful and beautiful at the same time.

"So I might need your help on Saturday, if you can spare any time for your old man," Max said once the room was completely deconstructed.

"What can I do?"

"Well, the gallery show opens on Saturday night. And it just occurred to me that I have no idea what the hell to wear."

"Why don't you wear what you always wear?" Celia said carefully, rolling up *Evening Fire*. "Keep it real."

198

"Stained army pants and a smock? Probably a little too real, even for an artist." Max tied string around *Lead Star* and stood up. "Want to take me shopping?"

Celia laughed. She used to constantly beg to take her dad out for some new clothes, but he'd always resisted, claiming that a true artist should care more about substance than style. In truth, Celia suspected, he'd always preferred to spend his money on new materials, not clothes. "Are you sure you don't want to go with Jane?" Celia teased.

"Oh, Jane doesn't have half your style and we both know it."

"True," Celia said. "Okay, we'll go on Saturday after I'm done with yoga. But you better be prepared to spend money."

"I've got money."

"Are you gonna spend it or are you going to get all cheap? Because I can't help you if you're not gonna help yourself."

"I'll spend the money," Max said grudgingly.

"Fine. This will be good." Celia thought for a second and then decided to press her luck. "You know, Dad, as long as we're out, I might as well get something new too. I mean, it's not every day my dad has a New York City gallery show, right? I should probably look pretty stylish myself."

Max chuckled and kissed her on top of her head. "Don't push it, kid," he said, stretching his arms on the way to bed.

Dr. Fein was a short, slim, worried-looking man; he reminded Junie of a jockey the day of an important race. He looked at her knee, asked about how the injury happened, and gently tried to turn the swollen joint until she shrieked with pain. "Sorry," he mumbled, taking notes. Next he sent her for some X-rays, and when the films were returned, Dr. Fein shook his head sadly. "You see?" he asked, pointing to a white space in her knee. "You tore your meniscus. Common runner's injury. Just as I suspected."

Ed put a comforting hand on her shoulder, but still Junie thought she might cry. She was going to need surgery after the school year ended. She'd never had surgery before.

Dr. Fein wrapped her knee, showed Ed how to help her with the bandage, and ordered a set of crutches for her from the medical supply facility down the hall. "You'll get a lot of attention," Dr. Fein said. "Everybody pays attention to the girl on crutches."

Ed dropped Junie off at home and then headed to a meeting in Manhattan. Junie crutched herself to the kitchen; next to the fridge she found a note in her father's handwriting—the word *Rob?* with a phone number. Rob. She still hadn't called him back. She picked up the phone and dialed Piccolo Dairy.

"Hey, Rob, it's Junie. I'm sorry I didn't get back to you yesterday. I had a bit of an injury." And she went on to tell him the whole stupid story, from the fall to the trainer to Dr. Fein.

"Man, that's terrible. Are you mobile? Do you want to come over and hang out?"

"Not at all, unfortunately," Junie said, a bit annoyed. Did he actually imagine that she'd want to go out? She had a torn meniscus! Her knee was a war zone of tears, cuts, and bruises! Guys were so insensitive. Junie said good-bye and turned on *The Price Is Right*.

Half an hour later the doorbell rang. Rob stood outside with flowers, chocolate, an Italian bread, and several wrapped hunks of cheese.

"You look great," he said, after kissing her on the cheek. "Not injured in the least."

"Thank you very much." Junie grinned, sticking her nose in the flowers. Gerber daisies and baby's breath; somehow he'd guessed her favorites. So much for the guy's insensitivity. It was too bad he stank of cigarette smoke.

Rob made her sit back down on the couch, arranged an afghan on top of her, and went to the kitchen to find a vase and a couple of plates. Junie lost herself in the Showcase Showdown, pulling the blanket up to her neck. When Rob returned, he had two grilled cheeses on a tray, with a vase of flowers in between.

"What's in the Showcase?" he asked, handing her a sandwich.

"The usual—a lawn mower, an outdoor grill, a new minivan. Nothing that I'd know what to do with . . . Oh my God, Rob, this sandwich is incredible."

"You like that?" He grinned and took a bite of his own. "It's fontina, melted on sourdough. A little romano on top. A couple of years ago I had mono and I swear this sandwich restored my strength."

"I can imagine." She tore into the sandwich. *The Price Is Right* ended with some girl in a college sweatshirt jumping up and down and kissing Bob Barker excitedly. She'd won the lawn mower–grill–minivan combo.

"Who's watching the store?" she asked when the first half was demolished.

"My father came in today," Rob said. "I think he's been feeling depressed since Maria died—he's been spending more time at the shop. It's good, though. I get to leave early and go home to write."

"What are you working on?"

"A short story," Rob said. Then, slyly, "About a guy who meets a girl."

"Is that so?" Junie asked. "What happens?"

"Not much," Rob said. "Until he kisses her."

This response struck Junie as a little bit cornball, but nevertheless Rob remained so cute (although was it her imagination or was he getting shorter?). Anyway, he'd brought her the flowers and all that food! So Junie put down her sandwich, and Rob put down his, and then he carefully adjusted himself around her bruised knee so that he could lean down and kiss her. The kissing was pretty nice. It wasn't as nice as the sandwich, though.

The phone rang just as he was unbuttoning her shirt. "I better get it," Junie said, reaching up for the phone. She expected it to be one of her parents or maybe a doctor with a date for the surgery.

"Junie?"

"Brian?"

"Hey," he said, and then was quiet for a second. Junie's heart sped up. What was Brian doing on the phone? He hadn't called her in so long. "I heard about your knee," he said after a moment.

"Yeah." Junie cast a guilty look over at Rob. He was leaning back on the couch, watching the twelve o'clock news broadcast, his mouth half open. She suddenly wished he'd disappear. "I'm going to need surgery in June. I tore my meniscus."

"Oh no. My brother did that a few years ago. The surgery's no big deal, but the recovery really blows."

"I know," Junie said. "I'm not looking forward to it." She longed to get up and take the phone to the kitchen, but she had no idea how to manage with both crutches and a phone. Rob just sat there like a stuffed animal, gazing at the television.

"It must have been a bad fall."

"Oh, I just got distracted."

There was no way she could have a normal conversation with Brian as long as Rob was on the couch. Still, they managed a bit of small talk, mostly about school and sports injuries. Brian had broken his collarbone playing lacrosse last year and sprained an ankle this season in soccer. Junie remembered it clearly; she'd brought him brownies and gave him a back rub to try to cheer him up.

Finally Brian took a deep breath. "I miss hanging out with you, Junie," he said. "I just thought you should know that."

"I know how you feel," Junie said, unable to say, "I miss you too," with Rob a foot away from her. Suddenly she remembered running in the rain through Green-Wood Cemetery, Brian at her side.

"Will you be at school tomorrow? Do you need anything now?"

"No, I'm pretty taken care of at the moment," Junie said. "But thanks for asking."

"Hey," Brian said, and his voice grew soft. "Anytime."

"I'll see you at school tomorrow. Thanks for calling, Brian." Junie quickly hung up, and Rob picked up his half of the sandwich and handed it to her. He didn't ask her who was on the phone, but he didn't get up to leave, either, and for some reason Junie really wished he would. "Want another sandwich?" he asked her.

"No thanks," Junie said. She couldn't imagine eating another bite.

Rob finally left an hour later, after two episodes of *Judge Judy*. At five-thirty Celia and Danielle came over with Max's old fondue set and a printed list of fondue-making instructions from the Internet. They had to do something with Rob's cheese, after all, and Junie's parents were both working in Manhattan; they wouldn't be home until late.

"Do you think Ed and Sue have something called kirsch?" Celia asked. "I think it's a kind of wine."

"Got it!" Danielle said. She seemed able to intuit her way to the liquor cabinet, pulling out a small red bottle of cherry brandy. "Cherries, yum."

"Yeah, my parents don't cook much, but they definitely like their cocktail hour."

While Junie sat at the counter and watched, Danielle chopped the cheese into cubes and Celia rubbed garlic over the inside of the fondue pot. Then they added the cheese and the kirsch, and Celia stood stirring while Danielle tried to figure out how to light the bottom part of the fondue set. "God, this would work so much better if we had a lighter."

"Too bad Rob went home. He'd definitely have a lighter. I think he's a big smoker, actually."

"He's been smoking since he was fourteen." Danielle laughed. "I get him a Zippo each year for his birthday."

"Why didn't you tell me?"

"I didn't realize it mattered." Danielle shrugged. "What, do you have asthma or something?" She lit a kitchen match and set the bottom part of the fondue set alight.

"No, that's not it . . ." Junie said, unable to pinpoint her objections. Was it because he lied about how often he smoked? Or was it just that smoking was such a turnoff? "I guess it's no big deal."

"Well, it's definitely nothing to freak out about," Danielle said, adjusting the fondue set's flame. "I can't believe people ever used these things on a regular basis."

"I think fondue's very retro chic," Junie said.

"Oh, please. You sound like Jane," Celia said, bringing the fondue from the stove top and placing it on the bottom part of the fondue set. "But now that I'm getting along with my dad a little better, I guess I dislike Jane a little less. And she did save my ass after I cut school."

"Amen to that," Danielle said.

The kitchen smelled delicious, like garlic and wine and cherries. The three set the fondue pot on the flame and crowded around it, tearing off pieces of bread and dipping them into the pot.

"So Rob just brought you all this cheese, huh?" Celia asked, while Danielle hummed, "Junie has a boyfriend," under her breath.

"He also brought me those flowers over there," Junie said, gesturing to the kitchen table. "And I know I should be feeling good about him right now. I mean, he's so sweet, and I think he really likes me."

"I *know* he really likes you," Danielle said, scooping up some cheeses.

Junie sighed guiltily. "Well, but then Brian called this afternoon and he said he misses seeing me. And I really miss him too. It's been a month without him, but I still think about him."

"You're kidding." Celia dropped a chunk of bread into the fondue. "So you've forgiven him his Amanda Begosian trespasses?"

"Well, look, it's not like we were even speaking at that point. And for some reason I was always madder at Amanda than I was at Brian."

"That's because we expect more from women than we do from men," Danielle said.

"Huh?" Junie looked up at Danielle mid-dunk.

"Female friendships are special. We expect our girlfriends to live up to a higher standard. Guys can get away with any old BS because, hell, they're guys. They think with their penises and can't help it."

"And I guess we forgive them for it," Junie said. The sky

was growing dim outside, but inside, the kitchen was bright and warm. Heat radiated from the bright blue fondue set, and the girls crowded closer around it.

Celia licked cheese from her fingertips. "I agree. Good female friendships are the strongest relationships in the world. And you know, I would sooner lose a guy than lose either of you."

"Speaking of, where's Henry been?" Danielle said, licking a finger.

"Oh, you know," Celia said. "I haven't seen as much of him lately." She hadn't told anyone about running away from his apartment, but all these secrets were weighing on her too heavily to stay quiet forever.

"Spill it, Cee. What's going on?"

Celia took a deep breath. She was in a kitchen with her two closest friends. Of course she could tell the truth. "Look, it's just that I've never been into a guy before, but I'm totally in love with Henry and I don't know what to do about it." There it was. Out there for the world to know. "It gets worse," she said. Junie and Danielle just stared at her. "Yesterday we were hanging out at his aunt's apartment, and I realized that I was totally falling in love with him, and then I ran out of his apartment like a deranged person."

"You didn't," Danielle said.

"I totally did," Celia said. "He probably thinks I'm such a freak."

"Why don't you call him and apologize?" Danielle said. "Tell him you got your period or something. Guys always believe the period excuse."

"No way," Celia said. "I can't face him."

"Hold up, hold up," Junie said. "I think we're all missing the point here. This is not about whether or not you ran out of Jane's house the other day. This is about the fact that you're into Henry and *you didn't tell us!*" She pelted Celia with a piece of rye.

"I was going to tell you." Celia laughed, ducking the bread. "I was just waiting for the right time."

Junie pelted her again. "What about 'I won't date no floppy-haired guys'? What about 'He has to be brilliant and respectful and taller than me'?"

Celia grabbed some bread from the basket and fired back, giggling. "Watch it, Goldstein," she said, but her bread hit Danielle by mistake. "Oops! Sorry!"

"Don't you dare, Celia Clarke!" Danielle shrieked, running to the counter and grabbing a bowl of grapes.

"No!" Celia scurried behind the kitchen table. Danielle chased after her, splattering her back with big green grapes. Junie, immobile, reached for a basket of dried apricots on the counter and began hurling them at both Celia and Danielle, who retaliated with almonds, peanuts, and cubes of Swiss cheese. Then Danielle got the Hershey's syrup out of the fridge (Sue had evidently visited Key Food today), and suddenly the stakes were high. Celia grabbed a jar of applesauce from the pantry. Junie reached for the only thing close by—a lukewarm handful of congealing fondue. The kitchen was silent for a moment as the girls eyed each other, assessing the danger. And then:

"Haaaaaaah!" Danielle screamed, spraying Hershey syrup at her opponents.

208

"No, you don't!" Celia scooped up applesauce and splattered it at both of them while Junie futilely attempted to fling melted cheese at her two friends. In a minute the kitchen became a Jackson Pollock of chocolate syrup, applesauce, cheese, nuts, and fruit. And Junie thought, as she ducked a flying peanut, that Danielle was right. Good female friendships were, without a doubt, the best friendships of all.

Fishnets and Letters

Just before her alarm went off, Junie had a vivid, last-minute dream. Amanda Begosian was in the backseat of a Rolls-Royce, steaming up the windows with Brian. Junie herself sat in the chauffeur's seat up front, driving them through the streets of Brooklyn, wearing a neat peaked cap and a dark suit. Periodically she'd point at the Manhattan skyline across the river, telling her passengers to look up at the Empire State Building or the Chrysler Building, but Amanda and Brian were too busy going at it to concentrate on anything but each other. As they were about to cross the Brooklyn Bridge, Chauffeur Junie could hear Brian say to Amanda, "You want to do it? I have a condom."

Junie woke up sweating, clutching her stuffed Chihuahua. She blinked twice and tried to put the dream out of her mind, but it was impossible. *I have a condom, I have a condom* played in her head as she gingerly showered, got dressed, brushed her hair, and ate her Corn Pops in the shade of the flowers Rob brought over the day before.

Seeing as how he was still in town, her father offered to drive her to school. Junie balanced her crutches across the backseat and stared out the window at the Manhattan skyline as it whizzed past them on their drive to Brooklyn Prep, thinking about her dream. She wondered what she should say to Brian if she saw him in school. Should she mention their phone call? Act like nothing had happened? Junie rested her head against the cool glass of the BMW's tinted window.

"You okay, sweetheart? Worried about the surgery?" Ed steered with one hand and used the other to fiddle with the radio. He liked to listen to the morning business reports.

"I'm fine," Junie said. The city hall building blurred past them. "I'm not really worried about the surgery. It's not until next month."

"That's my girl," Ed said. He put a hand on her good knee and patted it twice. "Everything's going to be just fine, you know. And your mom and I are going to stick around to see you through it."

"You are?" Junie asked.

"Princess, of course," Ed said, looking at her curiously. "You didn't really think we'd leave you before your surgery, did you?"

"No, of course not," Junie said, but secretly, until this moment, she hadn't been sure what her parents' plans were. She had been too afraid they'd leave soon to ask. *Distrust is a heavy burden,* she could hear Mrs. Finnegan whisper in her ear. *And you should never be afraid to ask for what you want. Who knows? You might even get it.*

"I'm glad you're staying, Dad."

Ed looked over at her and winked. "I am too."

Dr. Fein had been right about the popularity-to-crutches ratio. Junie was the belle of the Brooklyn Prep ball: everybody wanted to know what had happened to her, how she was feeling, if it was true she'd never run again. Amanda Begosian offered her a pathetic smile and helped her carry her bags from class to class, and when Coach passed her in the hall, she gave her a small hug. The attention actually felt pretty good, but the pain in Junie's knee wouldn't go away. Leaning against the mint green tiled walls of Brooklyn Prep's hallways, she popped three extra-strength Tylenols between history and French class and tried to soothe her stomach with a shot of the Pepto-Bismol she'd stashed in her backpack.

"You're like a one-woman pharmacy," said a familiar voice behind her. "Do you need some help getting to class?"

"Hey, Brian," Junie said, her heart pounding a little at the sight of him. He had let his stubble grow out the way she liked it, and he was wearing a dark gray long-sleeved T-shirt. He looked so good in dark colors. "Yeah, if you could take my bags, that'd be great."

Together they walked down the hall to Mrs. Lachelle's French 4 honors class. Junie had dispensation to be late because of the crutches, but she knew that Brian would be in trouble when he finally arrived in his history class. Still, she didn't hurry. It felt sort of nice to be walking at Brian's side again. Then she thought of Rob's flowers in the kitchen.

"So here we are," Brian said, outside Mrs. Lachelle's door.

"Thanks for the help."

"No problem."

Neither one of them made a move to leave.

"You know," Brian said, "I was wondering if maybe you wanted to get together this weekend and talk about stuff. No pressure or anything, but I thought . . ."

"My parents are in town this weekend, but we could meet up after school next week," Junie said. "Or whatever."

"Maybe Tuesday?"

"Sure," Junie said, taking her backpack from Brian's grasp. "That'd be good."

Brian bent down and softly kissed Junie's cheek. It was the barest of touches, but still it made her face burn. "Okay," he said. "I'll see you around." And then he drifted down the hall with that lazy walk of his, his Birkenstocks flopping against the floor. Junie leaned back against the hallway wall and took several deep breaths before heading into French.

After school on Friday, Danielle tore through her closet, trying to find the perfect top to wear with her St. Margaret's skirt, fishnet tights, and a pair of combat boots. The look she was going for was slutty-glam, a little Christina Aguilera and a little Courtney Love. She dug up an old black tank top with rivets around the neckline. She tied her hair up in messy knots on top of her head. The look was close, but not quite. She wished she had a tattoo. She still looked like too much of a good girl.

The remedy occurred to her as she was applying sparkly silver shadow—she needed her grandmother's crucifix! It was the ultimate goth accessory. Barreling down the stairs two at a time, Danielle rushed to Nonna's jewelry box to retrieve the massive silver crucifix her grandmother had worn at every Christmas and Easter. Danielle had never really liked the thing—it always seemed so heavy around her poor grandmother's neck—but she put it on and checked herself in Nonna's mirror, and she looked perfect.

"You look like a prostitute."

"Thank you very much," Danielle said. Her sister was standing by Nonna's doorway, her arms folded over her massive chest.

"But a cute prostitute," Christina said.

"Even better." Oh, Danielle thought, if only her sister would lose thirty pounds, start wearing different clothes, get a haircut. She had so much potential! Clear skin, nice brown eyes. But then again, what good was potential when your life's goal was to manage a lingerie department?

"Why are you taking Nonna's crucifix?"

"I'm just borrowing it."

"Borrowing from dead people is stealing." Christina sat herself on Nonna's faded damask bedspread. "Why are you dressed like that, anyway? Are you going out?"

"No, I'm not going anywhere. Just trying out a new look." Danielle sat down on the bed next to Christina and put her head on her shoulder, like she used to do when they were little girls and Christina was a full head taller than she was. "Don't you ever want a new look, Chris?"

"I like the way I look," Christina said. "I know you think I dress like an old lady, but I think you dress like a hooker, so maybe we're just a little bit limited in our perspectives."

"Don't get hostile."

"I'm not hostile." Christina sighed and then put her arm around Danielle's shoulders. "Anyway, you'll be glad to know I have a date tomorrow."

"Christina! You're kidding! With who?"

"This guy Michael. He's a regional sales manager. We've been checking each other out for months now, and finally he came up to lingerie this morning and asked me out. Right in front of everybody. For a real date, dinner and a show."

Dinner and a show, Danielle thought. That would be just the sort of dorky thing to turn Christina on. "Congrats, Chris. That's great. I hope he's a nice guy."

"Oh, he is," she said. "Cute, too. Well, a little bald, but basically very cute. I'm going to get a manicure in the morning." She paused, watching Danielle scratch at her knee. "Hey, can I ask you a question?"

"Sure."

"Have you ever gone through Nonna's dresser drawers?"

"What?" Danielle extricated herself from her sister's arm. "Why? Have you?"

"I asked first."

Christina's eyes gave nothing away, but Danielle knew she'd seen the letters. There was no other reason she'd be asking about Nonna's drawers. At the same time Danielle didn't want to admit too much. "After she died, I sort of went poking around. . . ."

"I did too," Christina said. Her eyes grew round. "And I happened to come across—"

"A package of Nonna's private stuff?"

"The letters?"

Danielle flopped back onto Nonna's heavy velvet pillows. "Yes," she said, gravely. "The letters."

"I almost died when I read them," Christina said. "I had always been under the impression that they had the happiest marriage imaginable. And the way that Nonna raved about him, like he was some kind of Prince Charming! But she knew the whole time. I did a little research, by the way. Asked Mrs. Lucci what she knew."

"You're kidding! That's so smart of you!"

"At first she didn't want to say anything—said it was all in the past, whatever—but evidently Lydia was a waitress at Uncle Joey's restaurant back in the day, the one he used to own over in Red Hook. She was Swedish, German, something like that. And she and our grandfather had an affair for ten years while Nonna was at home, taking care of mom and Uncle Sal. Ten years!"

"Ten years," Danielle repeated. "They must have really loved each other."

Christina shrugged. "Whether or not they loved each other was besides the point. He was married! To our *grandmother*!"

"True, true," Danielle said, embarrassed to be romanticizing her dead grandfather's adulterous affair.

"So evidently, Nonna finds these letters when she's dusting behind his bureau—Nonna used to *dust behind his bureau,* and still he cheated on her!—and anyway, the letters confirmed what she had suspected for years. So she takes the whole lot of them, marches over to Uncle Joey's, and tells Lydia to get the hell out of town. Immediately. And never come back, under threat of agony. Uncle Joey was backing her up."

"And did she?" Danielle asked. "Get the hell out of town?"

"Yep. Nobody ever saw her again. And from what Mrs. Lucci knows, Nonna and Grandpa never even talked about it. Not once. For the rest of both their lives."

"Oh my God."

"I know."

Christina was quiet for a moment, and then she crossed over to Nonna's drawer and withdrew the packet of letters. "The one thing that Mrs. Lucci asked is that we please not tell Mom. It was always very important to Nonna that Mom maintain her ideas about her father, that he was a good man, faithful, whatever."

"I wonder why she never threw the letters out," Danielle said.

"I asked Mrs. Lucci that, but she had no idea."

Danielle considered the enormity of this story. She tried to imagine her grandmother as a young woman, finding the letters, breaking down in tears, and then collecting herself to go find her husband's mistress. Telling her to get out of Brooklyn. Never mentioning it again.

Nonna was positively inspiring.

"Can I ask you a question, Chris?" Danielle asked, playing with the fringe on one of Nonna's pillows.

"Anything."

"Do you think that the women in our family are sort of cursed? Like we're all destined to end up with crappy men?"

"What do you mean?" The two girls were sitting on the bed cross-legged, the packet of letters between them.

"Well, Grandpa cheated on Nonna, and Dad ran off on Mom, and here I am dating morons like Steve—"

"Stop," Christina said. "Don't be silly. The situations are totally different. Mom and Nonna both married the first guys they ever dated, and that was years ago. You're not going to make that mistake, and neither am I. We're going to keep looking until we find guys who treat us like gold."

"But how do you know a guy's not going to turn into a jerk later?"

"I think you just choose as carefully as you can. Remember? That's what Nonna kept telling us: Be careful, *bambina*, be careful."

"Maybe this weekend's date will be the one."

"Maybe," Christina said, sprawling backward on the bed. "It would be nice. I haven't had a date in so long."

Danielle picked one of the letters out of the packet and held it between her fingers. The pink paper was yellowing with age, almost crumbling. If they had just left them in the drawer for a few more years, they'd probably soon be dust. "So what are we going to do with these?"

"I guess we should destroy them," Christina said. "Make

sure Mom never finds them. If Nonna was so good at keeping the secret when she was alive, we shouldn't let her blow it after she's dead."

"Okay," Danielle said, but she took the letter she'd been holding and set it aside. "But I think I'm going to keep just this one. Just to remember what Nonna warned me about."

So Danielle, still in her miniskirt and crucifix, and Christina, with her Macy's name tag still pinned to her blouse, went outside to the barbecue. They lit the charcoal, waited till the fire was nice and high, and then burned each of their dead grandfather's letters, except for one. Danielle imagined that they were burning the curse of the Battaglia women, no longer doomed to end up with lousy men.

"I feel like we should say something," Christina said as the fire ate each of the letters. "Like a prayer or something, I don't know."

Danielle shrugged and watched the smoke blow into the sky. "To our grandmother, Maria Bollino," she said. "May she rest in peace."

Lying across her bed in her favorite pink-and-silver kimono, Celia picked up the phone. It was ten-thirty at night. She dialed: 212-555-143—and then she quickly hung up. She tried again. 212-555-143 . . . Her finger hovered over the last digit, but she couldn't do it. She slammed down the phone, humiliation burning in her throat. But what was the point of calling Henry when she was so certain he'd never want to talk to her again?

Yellowtail,
Champagne,
and
Henry

Danielle couldn't believe how rad Celia looked. Breathtaking, gorgeous, dazzling, super-fly. She twirled around the living room in a tight cream-colored silk dress that fell to her knees, where it gently flared. It was cut low enough to show off the huge jade pendant that she wore around her neck; she had dusted on green glittery eye shadow in the same exact shade as the pendant. Her lips and nails were bright red, and on her feet she wore her trusty gold sandals.

"Do you like it?" she asked Danielle.

"You look like a model, I swear to God," Danielle said. "Like you should have your own reality show."

"It took me forever to talk my dad into buying this for me. We were in NoLita this afternoon and there was nothing else I liked and finally I just wore him down. All the girls in the store were like, C'mon, Dad, you've got to buy it for her! And eventually he pulled out his AmEx and here I am!"

"Good work," Danielle said. She herself had never been to a gallery opening and hadn't had the faintest idea of what to wear. She'd paced in front of her closet for almost an hour and in the end decided that black was probably the safest choice. So there she stood, in black pants, black heels, and a black short-sleeved T-shirt, and standing next to Celia, she felt as drab as an undertaker.

Junie arrived a few minutes later, wearing a chiffon skirt that floated gently over her knee brace. "Crutches, I know, very glamorous." She was holding a bag of sushi from Osaka on Court. "No soy sauce," she said. "Can't risk stains."

Dinner commenced with a ginger beer toast in honor of Max, who had beat a fast trail up to the gallery a few hours earlier in order to help set up. Reporters would be at the show and potential clients, and Celia claimed she had never seen her dad so nervous. Dressed in a new Prada suit, white shirt open, no tie, he stood at the living room door before he left and knocked back two quick shots of bourbon.

"So are you nervous about seeing Henry?" Danielle asked, wiping the wasabi off a piece of yellowtail. "He's gonna be there tonight, right?"

Celia shrugged and dissected her tuna roll with her chopsticks. "I guess so. But we haven't spoken since I ran out of Jane's apartment. I keep picking up the phone to call, but then I hit the second-to-last digit and hang up. I'm such a wimp."

"You're not a wimp, Cee," Junie said. She'd never thought of Celia as anything but brave and strong. "You're just in a weird spot."

"Listen, tonight you just got to go up to Henry and say

something," Danielle said. "Say anything! Play it like it's no big deal."

"But it is a big deal," Celia said, folding her napkin on her lap. She looked up at her friends helplessly. "It's a very big deal to me."

They took a car service to the Upper East Side, where the gallery was lit up with bright lights and beautiful people. (Danielle noted, to her relief, that most of them were also dressed entirely in black.) Max stood in the middle of the room among his sculptures as friends and colleagues swarmed around him.

"Celia!" he cried as the girls entered the gallery.

"Daddy!" Celia said, and allowed herself to be swept up in her father's enormous arms. She had promised herself she'd put Henry out of her mind—or at least try—and concentrate instead on her father's success. As she and Max hugged, a big-flashed camera took a picture.

"Now, don't you look wonderful, baby."

"So do you, Dad," Celia said. "I'm so proud of you."

"Anything sell yet, Max?" Junie asked.

"Darling, we have reserve orders on practically *everything*." Jane swooped up from behind, balancing on the highest, pointiest heels that Celia had ever seen. Her face was glowing with excitement, and her hair, for once, was long and loose over her shoulders. Pretty instead of garish.

"Wow, Jane," Danielle said. "That's really great."

"It's better than great, darling," Jane said. "It's *fabulous*." Beaming, she brushed up against Max and smooched him.

The crowd whooped and cheered, and the photographer's camera flashed.

"Get in the picture, Celia," Max instructed, and the photographer took another shot, Celia and Max and Jane squeezed together in an off-kilter hug.

As the photographer disappeared, Celia could sense a presence coming up behind her. A deep voice said, "Celia." She closed her eyes and turned around.

"Henry." She prayed he couldn't tell that her palms were starting to sweat, her heart starting to pound.

"Can I talk to you for a minute?" he asked. "In private?" She followed him to the far corner of the room, back behind *Burning Branches*. She could feel Danielle and Junie watching them and gave them a quick nod to let them know she was okay, even though she really didn't feel all that okay.

Henry and Celia stood for a moment facing each other in silence. He was wearing a dark shirt and a matching tie. His black eyes were glowing. Celia looked down at her sandals.

"So I've been spending the last three days trying to figure out what I did to make you run away," he said after another moment. "But no matter how much I think about it, I can't figure it out."

"I'm sorry," Celia said. She took a deep breath, kept staring at her sandals. "It was nothing you did. I don't know what came over me. I just needed to get some air, I guess. I was feeling a little—um, light-headed."

"I see. Light-headed."

"I'm really sorry," Celia said glumly. She couldn't tell if

Henry was really mad or just confused. Either way, it made her miserable.

"Celia, the way you ran off—I just didn't know what to think. And then you didn't call to explain, so I figured you didn't want to talk to me anymore."

"Look," Celia said, meeting his glare. "I wanted to call you, I really did, but I was too embarrassed for having run away. . . ."

Henry sighed and put his hands in his pockets. His eyes were cloudy, unreadable. "Well, as long as you're not mad at me."

"Henry—" Celia started, but then she stopped. She could feel the words bubbling up in her throat; all she had to do was open her mouth and they'd come pouring out. *Henry, I had to run away from you because I think I'm falling in love with you and this has never happened to me before and I don't know what to do about it and I'm scared to death. Kiss me, would you?*

"Celia? Are you all right?"

Celia clamped her lips shut and nodded, afraid of what she was about to say. Out of nowhere a bright light flashed, making her eyes water. "Smile, you two!" The photographer.

"Right, then." Henry put his arm around her, as though there was no tension between them at all. He smelled so good. His body was so warm.

They both smiled, and the photographer took one shot, then another, then another. "You two are a gorgeous couple," he said before he moved on to take a picture of *Three Friends.*

Couple. That word again. Celia looked up at Henry to

see if he'd caught it; clearly he had, since his cheeks had gone pale.

"Oh, *there* you are!" Jane tottered over, her face glowing, her breath smelling of a bit too much champagne. "I was wondering where you two were hiding! Come now, don't be party poopers! Come join the rest of the crowd!" And she grabbed both Henry and Celia's hands and dragged them toward the middle of the party, with all the noise, and the cocktails, and the bright, flashing lights. Celia tried to make conversation with some of her father's colleagues, but she found it hard to concentrate. Henry disappeared to go talk to the DJ.

"You okay, Cee?" It was Danielle, eating a slice of brie off a grease-stained cocktail napkin.

"Yeah," Celia said. "Henry and I talked about what happened."

"And?"

"And . . . and I guess it'll be okay."

"Did you tell him that you like him?" Danielle asked with her usual impatience.

"Jesus, girl, are you kidding? I could barely eke out an apology, much less a confession."

"But he's leaving in a few days, Cee!"

"I know, Danielle, I know," Celia said. "How could I forget?"

Danielle swallowed her brie and balled up the napkin as if to change the subject. "Well, I just wanted to tell you that Junie's outside, resting her knee. We're going to take a cab home together—her injury's killing her and I don't want her to go home alone."

"Sure, that's cool." Celia gave Danielle a quick hug and then watched her friend disappear. Max and Jane were in the middle of yet another crowded conversation, and the gallery-goers swarmed around her without pausing. Celia applied some fresh lipstick just to look busy.

"Let's get out of here."

"What?" It was Henry, holding a glass of wine.

"The party's dying down. It's time to go."

"Go where?" Celia said, dropping her lipstick on the floor. Were her hands really trembling?

Henry bent down and picked the lipstick up. "Back home, love."

So they said their good-byes to Max and Jane (who were going downtown for a post-party celebration) and headed out into the cool night, Celia's hands clasped to keep from shaking.

"Jane's apartment has lovely views at night," Henry said. They walked to Jane's building in silence, occasionally exchanging the briefest nervous glances. Celia wondered if Henry had any plans or if he was just improvising. The breeze felt cool and gentle on her face.

When they got to Jane's apartment, they were greeted by anxious barks.

"Shhh, shhh, Ginger, it's just us," Henry said, locking Jane's door behind him as the dog bounced up and down at their feet. Celia picked up Ginger and petted her, suddenly a bit more nervous. What was going to happen now?

Henry turned on the lights and put a CD in Jane's stereo—good music this time. Billie Holiday. "What, did you think I was going to play Ninja Star?"

"So what are we doing here, anyway?"

"Looking at the view," Henry said. "Remember?"

So together they stood in front of the south-facing window, where all of New York City was lit up before them. Henry put his hands on her shoulders. She held her breath.

"Celia, why don't you put Ginger back on the floor?"

"Okay," she whispered.

And then he kissed her.

"Is that okay?" he asked.

It was as good as she had dreamed, as good as she ever dared to hope. His lips were warm and soft, and his fingers brushed the back of her neck gently. Celia felt her hands stop trembling, her heart stop racing. She relaxed in his arms. "It's wonderful," she said. She was home.

They curled up on the couch and kissed for hours. Celia's new dress wrinkled under his hands. She tried to memorize exactly what his skin felt like, exactly what his lips tasted like so that when he went away, she'd still be able to close her eyes and remember all this.

"Please come see me in London," Henry said.

"As soon as I have summer break," Celia said. "In just a few weeks." She'd figure out how to talk Max into it. Hell, she'd managed to talk him into buying her the dress (now a damp and sweaty mess, oh well).

When they finally stopped kissing, their lips felt bruised and sore, and their cheeks were flushed. The birds had started chirping outside, a sign that the sun was due to rise. Celia looked out at the view of Central Park, hoping her dad was too busy celebrating to notice that it was way past curfew.

Meteors,
Heartbreak,
and
a Turquoise Bracelet

Sunday morning, Danielle sat in her bathrobe, drinking grapefruit juice and gazing at the Sunday edition of the *Daily News*. Jennifer Lopez bought a new mansion. The Mets lost again. Sanitation workers were angry about working conditions. Blech. She folded the newspaper in half and had gotten up to take a shower when she heard the front door open. In walked Christina, wearing last night's clothes and an enormous grin.

"And where have you been, young lady?" Danielle asked.

"I had a date, remember?"

"Oh my God," Danielle said. "Tell me you did not spend the night with your date."

Christina refused to answer, just sashayed into the room, dropping her purse on the floor.

"Answer me right now, Christina Battaglia. Tell me you did not spend the night with him."

"Shhh!" Christina said, biting her lower lip. "Mom might be home."

"Mom's at church. What happened? Did you sleep with him?"

"Nah," Christina said. "I mean, I spent the night, but we didn't sleep together. We just stayed out until three in the morning and he lives in Manhattan, so . . ."

"What did you do all night?" Danielle was dazzled. Christina spent the night at a boy's house! This was like meteor-hitting-the-earth unexpected.

"Ahhh . . ." Christina slid out of her heels and leaned against the refrigerator. "First we went for dinner," she said dreamily. "It was this cute French place in the theater district, and I don't know that much about French food, but Michael told me what everything was and it was *so good.* And then we went to see *The Lion King,* which was amazing, and then we went for drinks and didn't get back to his apartment until three. He wants to see me again this week. He wants to be my boyfriend." Christina's blouse was untucked, and she had red-wine stains on her teeth.

"Get out of here!" Danielle jumped from her chair to give her sister a hug. "Oh, Chris, that's so great. I can't wait to meet him. Mom's going to be so excited! Do you think Nonna would have liked him?"

"Nonna," Christina said, "would have loved him." Sighing again, still dreamy, Christina sailed out of the room and up the stairs, shedding her date clothes as she went. In a minute Danielle heard the shower start up. So Christina had a boyfriend.

Better watch for meteors.

*　　*　　*

Henry's flight left at 8:30 P.M. Monday, which meant that he had to leave for JFK at five. Celia sped out of school the second the bell rang, but the subways were slow and cramped all the way to the Upper East Side. "Let's go, please, please, let's go," she whispered like a prayer. She would never forgive herself if she missed Henry.

The conductor got on the subway to apologize for the delay, for which he blamed traffic on the 6 line. Celia cursed under her breath. "Let's go let's go let's go." She took deep meditative breaths to slow her heart. Henry was leaving. She stood crowded between a fat man who smelled like butter and a tall, fidgety woman with a miniature dachshund in a bag under her arm. He was leaving and she didn't know when she'd see him again.

As she clutched the subway's handrail, she let her memory revisit Saturday night. Henry kissing her, Henry holding her, Henry rolling around on the couch with her.

The subway started humming along, then stopped with a bump, then started again. Four-eleven. Let's go let's go let's go let's go.

At four twenty-five, knots tight in her stomach, Celia raced out of the Eighty-sixth Street station and across the avenues to Jane's apartment. The doorman opened the door for her and she ran to the elevator without even checking in.

"You're here," Henry said. He was in the living room, packing his records into a large canvas case. "I was afraid you weren't going to make it."

"So was I," Celia said. He looked so beautiful, dark hair

falling in his eyes. She was even starting to love his stupid neon windbreaker. "Where's Jane?"

"Walking the dog," Henry said. He sat down on the couch and opened his arms for her to cuddle into him. "We have a few minutes, though."

"I can't believe all we have is a few minutes," Celia said, not even bothering to try not to sound cheesy. "These were the fastest three weeks of my life."

"Are you going to miss me?" he asked.

"You have no idea." She kissed him on the ear. Even now her stomach was clenched, but not in sadness so much as anticipation: soon he would be leaving, and she'd better adjust. She took one of his hands and pressed it against her own.

"You know, I never would have believed that I could get this freaked out over a boy," she said. "See what you've done to me? I used to be the coolest girl in Brooklyn, and now you're leaving and I'm a basket case."

"I wish I didn't have to go home."

"So then stay."

"My DJ gig," Henry said. He kissed her fingers. "But you'll visit, yeah?"

"Of course," Celia said. "I'll figure out a way to convince my dad to let me go."

"That's a love," Henry said. When he was gone, who would call her "love"?

They started kissing, Celia kissing Henry harder and harder to keep herself from completely freaking out. She wound her fingers in his hair. She kissed his neck. The clock was ticking loudly over their heads, and Jane could arrive back home at any second.

And then she did.

"Hellooo! Hellooo!" she called, her heels clicking audibly from the front hall. "I'm back, darling! Henry, you better be all packed!"

Celia and Henry pulled away from each other, their faces red and flushed. "You mean it? I'll see you this summer?"

"Of course," Celia said, and leaned in to give him one final real kiss.

The good-byes themselves were rushed and confused: Ginger yapping, Jane nattering, and a bellman waiting to carry Henry's bags downstairs. Henry, the bellman, Jane, Celia, and Ginger all piled into the elevator, which was already crowded with Henry's suitcases and boxes of brand-new musical equipment.

"You will call me when you get back, won't you, darling?"

"Of course, Jane," Henry said. Crammed together in the corner of the elevator, he and Celia were squeezing each other's hands.

"And tell your mum I said hello," Jane said as the elevator doors opened, depositing them all in the sumptuous lobby. The bellman dragged Henry's baggage to the curb, where a long black car was waiting. Jane busied herself fixing Ginger's collar to give Henry and Celia a half moment of privacy.

"Bye," Celia whispered, wrapping her arms around him.

"Right, then," Henry said, kissing Celia on the cheek. "I'll see you soon."

"Of course you will," Celia said. She could feel her eyes growing foggy with tears.

"Don't cry, love," Henry said, but his voice was breaking.

Jane stopped fussing with Ginger and gave her nephew a peck on the cheek. "Fly safe, darling. And remember to hydrate on the plane. Lots of water. It's terribly dry up there, recycled air, simply horrid for the lungs."

"Right, Auntie Jane," Henry said as the bellman closed the car door.

As they watched the long black car ease into Upper East Side traffic, Celia thought that she could have accompanied him to the airport. She could have taken the subway home after his plane left. She could have bought herself another few hours with Henry.

But in the end the result would have been the same: he'd fly across the ocean, and she'd remain exactly where she was.

"Don't look so woebegone, darling," Jane said when Celia went back into the apartment to collect her book bag. "You'll see him again soon."

"Do you think my dad will let me go?"

"I'll do my best to talk him into it," Jane said. "It would be lovely if you could visit the boy. I've never seen my nephew this happy, you know."

"For real?"

"Of course, my dear. Why would I lie?"

And before Celia could stop herself, she leaned down to give Jane an enormous hug. For a moment or two Jane hugged back. Celia could feel the tears leaking out of her eyes, and Jane must have felt them too.

"All right, all right, Celia. That's quite enough now, darling, don't muss the hair. . . ."

Celia laughed and, wiping her eyes, hugged Jane even
harder.

Brian was waiting for Junie on her front stoop, and the sight
of him there was jarring. They used to meet on the stoop as a
matter of course, but it had been over a month since he'd
shown up in her part of Brooklyn. He was listening to his
iPod turned up full blast. She could hear it through the
headphones: a bootleg recording of the Dead.

Junie hobbled out and sat down next to him on the top
step. It was a windy May afternoon, and although the sky
was blue, the air had suddenly taken an unseasonably chilly
turn. Junie was wearing one of her father's old sweatshirts
and a pair of nylon racing pants over her knee brace. She
hadn't bothered to get pretty for Brian's arrival. Hell, he
knew what she looked like. But she had clasped on the
turquoise bracelet he'd given her, for old times' sake.

"So what are you listening to? One of the Red Rocks
concerts?"

"*New Year's at the Oakland Coliseum*," Brian said, taking
off the headphones. "The one with the ten-minute 'Terrapin
Station.'"

"I know," Junie said. *New Year's at the Oakland Coliseum*
was one of Brian's favorite make-out CDs.

"It's nice to see you," he said, and bumped her gently with
his shoulder. "How are you feeling? How's the knee?"

"Not so bad. Plus my parents are staying home with me,

so they've been driving me to school and stuff. Making sure my painkiller prescription stays up-to-date."

"That's important," Brian said.

"You have no idea."

They were silent then, and Junie discovered that it was hard to relax sitting next to him. She thought about what Celia would advise: long, slow breaths from the abdominal wall right up through the diaphragm. She inhaled through her nose and exhaled through her mouth.

"You okay?" Brian asked. "You're breathing funny."

"Listen, what did you want to talk about, anyway?"

"Ummm . . ." Brian looked down, fiddled with the controls on his iPod. "Okay, well, I guess you know about that stupid thing that happened with Amanda."

"Of course I know," Junie said. "I'm not an idiot."

"Well, basically I wanted to apologize for that. We were drunk and at this party and I wasn't thinking—"

"You know what, Brian? I've heard it all already and it doesn't concern me anymore. It's between you and Amanda." Junie watched as the wind kicked up a small whirlwind of leaves and then scattered them at the foot of the stoop. "What I really want to know is why you stopped talking to me in the first place. That was the thing that really hurt."

"Because you kept pushing me away," Brian said. "And then when I saw that you'd stopped wearing my bracelet, it just became crystal clear. You didn't want to be with me anymore."

"Brian, I tried to tell you, that whole bracelet thing was a mistake, a total misunderstanding—"

"Yeah, but I don't really believe in misunderstandings," Brian said. "Not like that. You took it off because you didn't want to wear it anymore, and that's all I needed to know."

Junie closed her eyes, and they sat there in awkward silence for another minute. "I didn't mean to push you away, Brian. I just don't think I was as ready to get serious as you were. And I kind of freaked out. But I'm wearing the bracelet now," she said, pushing up her sleeve to show him.

"That's cool," he said, but he looked a little embarrassed, so Junie rolled her sleeve back down. She knew what he was thinking: too little, too late.

"Look," he said. "I didn't mean to get back at you by, you know . . . that thing with Amanda. That was wrong. I'm sorry."

"Well," Junie said, "I understand. It's okay."

She wanted to tell him about learning to cook with her friends. She wanted to tell him about getting drunk and puking on that guy at that party in Williamsburg. She wanted to tell him how depressed she was to be missing track camp this summer. She wanted the old Brian back, her boyfriend, her friend, the person she could tell anything to. Maybe someday she would. "I'm sorry too."

Together they sat and watched the leaves. The little girl from across the street wheeled her bicycle along the side-walk. "So was that all you wanted to talk about?" she said.

"I guess so," Brian said. "Also . . . I was hoping we could talk in the halls again. It sucks not to talk to you, Junie."

"I know," Junie said. "I miss talking to you too."

So Brian helped lift Junie up by the arms, and just for a

second he was close enough for her to smell his familiar soapy smell. He walked her to the door, holding her arms, and handed her the crutches. She thought for a second he might kiss her cheek again, but instead he pulled away.

"Say hi to your parents for me, okay?" he said.

"Sure," Junie said. "Say hi to yours."

"Cool," Brian said. "I'll talk to you tomorrow." And as she watched Brian lope down the street, Junie was surprised to find herself smiling. She remembered what Mrs. Finnegan said the first time she'd met him: *I have a nice feeling about that Brian. He's going to make you happy in the end.* Junie suspected that once again, Mrs. Finnegan would turn out to be right.

Back inside the house, Sue was going through paperwork at the small desk in the kitchen. "You okay?"

"Yeah," Junie said. "A little tired. The painkillers knock me out."

"Rob called." Sue put down her notebook and looked up at Junie. "I told him you'd call him later tonight."

"Thanks," Junie said. Rob. He was such a nice guy and such a good kisser—exactly the person to turn to after Brian disappointed. But he was the last person she wanted to talk to. Right now she wanted her friends.

Sue passed her the phone, and Junie called Danielle and then she called Celia to arrange a much-needed girls' dinner for Friday night.

Junie,
Celia,
and
Danielle

"Look, just promise me we'll be done with dinner by ten."

"We'll be out of here by ten, Danielle. What's your problem?"

It was a quarter to six, and Danielle and Celia were bustling around the Battaglia kitchen with aprons tied around their necks. Underneath the apron Celia was wearing silk cargo pants and a tank top, but Danielle was dressed more conservatively—a long denim skirt and a dark blouse. Weirdly prudish, Celia thought.

Junie sat at the table, chopping garlic. "How many people are coming again?"

"We've got twelve, including us," Celia said.

"Actually, thirteen."

"Who's the thirteenth?" Junie asked, mincing the garlic into a small white mound.

"I told Rob to come. Last minute. He was bringing ricotta

for my mother anyway and I thought you wouldn't . . ."

"Oh no," Junie said. She had never actually called Rob back the other day, or too many of the days before that. It was tough—it wasn't like he had done anything wrong, exactly; in fact, he'd done almost everything right. But Junie still couldn't deal with him right now.

"Well, you would have had to face him eventually," Celia said. She was flush with the wisdom of a woman in love.

"Just don't break his heart, okay?" Danielle said. She was sautéing onions in a wide iron skillet. "Rob's family."

"I know," Junie said. "I'll do my best."

The menu tonight was a collection of girls' dinner classics: tagliatelle with tomato gravy, an arugula salad, Nonna's eggplant rollatini, sautéed shrimp, caramelized oranges, and garlic bread. The guests included Mrs. Lucci, Max and Jane, Ed and Sue, Rita and Christina, and Christina's new boyfriend. And Shrub, of all people. And Rob.

Christina helped set the dining room table, pulling out leaves so that it was extended to its full twelve-plus seating capacity. She'd brought home new porcelain plates using her discount from Macy's; it was time, she'd announced, to throw Nonna's moldy old china away. Rita didn't protest. Times were changing whether she was ready for them or not.

Rita attempted to re-create Nonna's famous tiramisu, using chocolate shavings and crushed Italian ladyfinger cookies. "I should have watched my mother more carefully," she said, stirring marsala wine into the mascarpone. "I never thought she'd abandon me without teaching me how to make a proper tiramisu. Do you think this is too much wine?" She licked her finger and poured a little more in.

At seven o'clock the guests started to arrive: first Max and Jane, who made an enormous show of admiring the heavily framed portraits and the old velvet drapes. "It's just so *rare* to see such character in furnishings anymore!" she said, begging the flattered Rita to give her the full tour of the house. Celia could hear her exclaim over the ancient oak furniture in the sitting room. "Darling, this would earn you a positive *fortune* at auction. Let me know if you're ever interested." No matter what kind of affection Celia could now find for Jane in her heart, she was still totally cringeworthy.

Sue and Ed showed up next, warmly greeting the girls, Christina, and Max. Ed had long been interested in buying one of Max's sculptures—"and now that I'm in New York for more than three days in a row, I'll finally be able to come take a look at your work." Jane swooped in from the sitting room to give him her gallery card.

Shrub arrived next, looking freshly scrubbed and a little spaced out ("Tell me you didn't smoke up before having dinner *with my family,*" Danielle whispered gruffly), followed by Mrs. Lucci ("Is this your new boyfriend, Danielle? He looks much, much nicer than that other degenerate!"). Next came Michael, Christina's date, holding a red rose for her in his hands. He was a little bit chubby and slightly balding, but his smile was genuine and his eyes were kind. He shook everybody's hand courteously and helped Christina pass out drinks—wine or ginger beer, depending on age and temperament.

Finally, just as the girls were getting ready to serve, the final guest arrived. It was Rob. With a slightly defeated look on his face he cornered Junie in the kitchen, where she was arranging garlic bread on a platter. "Hey, stranger."

"Hi," Junie said, flooded with a wave of guilt and embarrassment. He was still cute, still sweet, still generous and helpful. But she didn't want to be anyone's girlfriend right now. Brian knew it, and so did she. Junie Wong-Goldstein, lone wolf.

"So you haven't been returning my calls."

"I know," she said. "I'm so sorry. It's not like it's anything you've done, but I'm just sort of overwhelmed with stuff right now and I—"

"So it's not you, it's me? That kind of thing?"

"I guess so," Junie said. "I'm sorry." She looked down at the slices of bread with the golden garlic spread out on them. Her knee started to throb.

"Hey," Rob said. "Don't look so upset! I'll live. Although I would be lying if I said I wasn't disappointed."

"Rob, I really feel bad about everything. It's just that there's so much going on with me right now and I—"

"Hey," he said. "No hard feelings." He took the platter from her and carried it into the dining room, and she followed him on her crutches, wondering if she'd ever meet such a nice guy again and thinking, just for a second, that it was possible she was really blowing it.

"So here's a toast to the ladies!" Max stood with a wineglass full of ginger beer in his hand. "May you keep on cooking together for years to come."

"Hear, hear!" said the assembled crowd before digging into

the meal. The tagliatelle was perfect—al dente, with tomatoes and plenty of basil and a splash of the best green olive oil. Celia had sautéed the shrimp head-on with garlic and lemon, causing Jane to shriek in delight. "Oh, prawns! This is just *divine!*" The caramelized oranges were snappy and sweet, the eggplant rollatini miraculously crisp and soft at the same time. Even the dressing for the arugula salad was pitch-perfect, a simple mix of raspberry vinegar, oil, and mustard.

"So I'd like to mention that the last time Junie cooked for me, it was burnt scrambled eggs on Mother's Day," Sue said to Mrs. Lucci, who was sitting on her left. "Ten years ago."

"Well, now that you're home for a while," Junie said, "I'll cook for you more often. Right, Dad?"

"Right," Ed said, his mouth full of tagliatelle.

"Modern girls." Mrs. Lucci sighed, forking eggplant into her mouth. "They're so wrapped up in boys these days, in clothing, in their careers. They don't have time to think about what really matters anymore. Like learning to cook for a family."

"I hate to argue with you, Mrs. Lucci," Christina said, "but isn't it possible that women should aim for something higher than just cooking and cleaning at home?"

Mrs. Lucci shook her head sadly, as though she were listening to heresy, but Danielle was delighted at her sister's outspokenness. Michael was sitting next to her, and Danielle imagined that he had his hand on her knee. She hoped that he was the kind of guy who would push Christina to achieve. Even if achievement just meant climbing the Macy's hierarchy.

"So school's ending soon for you ladies, isn't it?" Rita said, helping herself to another piece of eggplant.

"What are you going to do this summer, Junie?" Celia asked. "I mean, after the surgery. You'll have no track camp for the first time in years."

"I talked to George about getting a Hamptons share this July," Ed said, refilling his wineglass. George was his partner at the consulting firm. "I thought it would be a nice place for you to recuperate. And I'll be working from the Manhattan office this summer, so I'll be able to get out to the beach every weekend."

"They have great produce out in the Hamptons," Max said. "All those farmers' markets. It's a good place to learn to cook."

"Are we off to the beach then this summer, lovey?" Jane asked. *Lovey?* Junie, Danielle, and Celia mouthed simultaneously.

"What do you think, Cee? Feel like going to the beach this summer?"

"Actually, Dad, I was planning on visiting London this summer."

"By yourself?" Max put on a skeptical smile. "Why don't we talk about it after dinner?"

Celia nodded. Talking about it after dinner was an important first step.

Before they knew it, the plates were empty, the dinner dishes were cleared, and Nonna's tiramisu-by-way-of-Rita appeared and vanished in minutes. Dinner was over. It was nine-fifteen.

"So are we going now or what?" Shrub asked Danielle.

"Going where?"

"Um, there's a show . . ." Danielle said. Under her blouse she could feel the riveted tank top sticking to her chest. She was sweating. "At the Rattletrap."

"Not Steve Reese's band," Christina said, sounding worried.

"Um, well, not exactly." She and Shrub stood at the same time. In her pocket she fingered Nonna's crucifix.

"Can we come?" Celia asked.

"You girls go ahead," Rita said. "Us old people will do the dishes."

"You sure?" Junie asked, already reaching for her crutches.

"Sure, we're sure." Sue was scraping her tiramisu bowl with her spoon. "You guys did the cooking, so we'll do the cleaning up. It's only fair."

"Right," Celia said.

"Right," Junie said. She looked over at Rob, who was playing with his napkin. "You coming?"

"I better be getting back, actually. I've got some writing to do."

"Really?" Junie said, but Rob didn't look up—just sat there, playing with his napkin. "Okay," she said quietly.

The girls kissed their respective parents good-bye and trooped out of the house. Shrub rushed ahead, toward Smith Street and the Rattletrap. "Gotta do the sound check," he yelled over his shoulder.

"See ya," Danielle called, and then stopped by the bushes at the edge of Fourth Place. She took a quick look around to make sure nobody but her friends was watching and then unbuttoned her blouse and threw it under the bushes.

"Damn," said Celia. "I was wondering why you were wearing that ugly-ass shirt. That tank top is so hot!"

"Shhh . . ." Danielle said, shedding her baggy skirt to reveal the black mini. She had Nonna's crucifix in her palm. "Do you mind putting this on me?" she asked, handing it to Celia.

Junie leaned on her crutches, admiring her friend's transformation. "You're going to sing tonight, aren't you?" She already knew the answer.

Danielle just nodded. Her eyes were bright. Celia finished affixing the necklace and tousled Danielle's hair for effect. She looked every inch the hard-core rocker chick: messy hair, fishnet tights, silver crucifix glowing in the dark. "I can't believe it, but I'm actually going to sing onstage. With the band. Steve's band. And he doesn't even know it yet."

"Oh my God! He's going to completely freak out." Junie laughed. "This is the best revenge—to show him up on his own turf."

Danielle smiled shyly. "Hey, Cee—did I ever thank you for standing up for me? I can't remember, with all that drama—"

"No apology necessary," Celia said, hugging Danielle in a gigantic embrace that tousled her hair even more. "So are you nervous?"

"I'm not nervous," Danielle said, but then she bent down to scratch her knee. "Okay, maybe I'm a little nervous. But you know—it sounds cheesy, but I really believe that you guys give me strength. As long as you're cheering for me, I know I'll be okay."

"Oh my God, Danielle, we'll be screaming our heads off," Junie said. Was it her imagination or were her eyes starting to water? She wiped them quickly with the back of her hand.

"You ready?" Celia asked.

"Ready," Junie and Danielle said at the same time, smiling at each other.

And then the three girls turned down Smith Street toward the Rattletrap. Junie balanced on her crutches, Celia marched in her gold sandals, and Danielle sang quietly to warm up her voice, under the streetlights of Brooklyn, where they belonged.

Acknowledgments

I'm so grateful for the patience and wisdom of Ben Schrank, for his friendship and for his ceaseless and wonderful work on *Girls Dinner Club*. Thanks also to the fine people at Alloy Entertainment who helped make this novel happen. Thanks always to my family for their confidence and their love, and to Ben Freeman for happily eating a hundred *Girls Dinner Club*–inspired meals. I owe an enormous debt of gratitude to Lexa Hillyer and Abigail McAden, for their guidance, their terrific insights, and their amazing dedication to this novel. Thank you also to Margo Lipschultz for her tireless enthusiasm, and to Stephanie Posen for her terrific advice. And finally, thanks to Julie Barer, as always, for everything.